*B*ehold, he sendeth an invitation unto all men, for the arms of mercy are extended towards them, and he saith: Repent, and I will receive you.

—Alma 5:33

Chosen

Chosen

The Path to Divine Acceptance

By

Steven A. Cramer

CFI
Springville, Utah

ISBN 13: 978-1-59955-028-2

Published by CFI, an imprint of Cedar Fort, Inc., 2373 W. 700 S., Springville, UT, 84663
Distributed by Cedar Fort, Inc. www.cedarfort.com

LIBRARY OF CONGRESS CATALOGING-IN-PUBLICATION DATA
Cramer, Steven A.
  Chosen : the path to divine acceptance / Steven A. Cramer.
    p. cm.
  ISBN 978-1-59955-028-2
  1. Mormon missionaries--Fiction. 2. Spiritual warfare--Fiction. 3. Religious fiction. I. Title.

PS3603.R366C48 2007
813'.6--dc22

                    2007005413

Cover design by Nicole Williams
Edited and typeset by Annaliese B. Cox
Cover design © 2007 by Lyle Mortimer

Printed in the United States of America

10 9 8 7 6 5 4 3 2 1

Printed on acid-free paper

Contents

Acknowledgments

I express gratitude to my publisher, Lyle Mortimer, who not only suggested the subject and purpose of this book but also cared enough about the project to keep insisting until I finally agreed to do it.

I am indebted to President Spencer W. Kimball for the foundation and standards that he taught in his landmark book *The Miracle of Forgiveness*, which I used extensively for this project.

I appreciate my wife's brother, D. Chad Richardson, for his time and support. First, for his invaluable input in clarifying the relationships between missionaries and their mission presidents. And second, my deepest gratitude for allowing me to share excerpts from his moving article on how to forgive and view ourselves after repentance without applying the typical self-deprecating labels that so many of us mistakenly attach to ourselves (see chapter thirty-one).

I am particularly grateful to my dear wife, LoAnne, whose editing skills often challenge my author's ego but always make my writing better than I ever could have done on my own.

And many thanks, of course, to the various members of the staff at Cedar Fort for their invaluable help in producing the finished product.

Introduction

One day as I walked down a hallway in the temple, I saw a little spider walking along the carpet. Startled, I thought, *What are you doing here? You don't belong here!* Immediately, the thought came into my mind that I should live in such a way that a higher Being than I might not look down upon *me* and say, "What are *you* doing here? You don't belong here!" I decided again, for the umpteenth time, that I would live so as to be worthy of being chosen and accepted. However, like many people, I felt deep inside that my frequent and continuing need of repentance diminished my hope of being chosen.

When I thought about the lives of others who are seemingly more righteous than I, I wondered how I could ever be chosen to receive the same glory that they will receive. Yet, I knew that such self-defeating attitudes of doubt are not productive nor pleasing to the Lord, for "man must hope, or he cannot receive an inheritance in the place which [God] hast prepared" (Ether 12:32).

One thing that made me question my chances of being chosen was the haunting statement in scripture that says, "Many are called, but few are chosen" (see Matthew 20:16; 22:14; D&C 95:5; 121:34, 40). Misunderstanding its meaning, I concluded that, in comparison to others, such as prophets and apostles, I was far behind and had little chance.

One of the first clues that I had misunderstood the meaning of those "few are chosen" scriptures was a statement made by Elder Bruce R. McConkie in a training session to about five hundred Church Educational System teachers in Salt Lake City, Utah. One of the teachers asked him: "How do we keep our students from being discouraged (and how do we avoid discouragement ourselves) when we read in the scriptures that strait is the gate and narrow is the way that leads to life and few there be that find it?" BYU Professor Robert L. Millet reported this response: "I will never forget Elder McConkie's powerful but totally unexpected answer. He stood up straight at the pulpit and stated, *'You tell your students that far more of our Father's children will be exalted than we think!'* "[1]

As I analyzed the five scriptural passages containing the phrase, "many are called, but few are chosen," it became obvious that, rather than making a generalized statement about the slim chances of mankind making it back to Him, the Lord was referring to some very specific reasons that could cause us to become un-chosen. To keep it in context, many verses testify that every one of us has been invited and are already chosen to return to His presence to dwell with Him eternally. For example, Mormon taught, "Thus we see that the gate of heaven is open unto all, even to those who will believe on the name of Jesus Christ, who is the Son of God" (Helaman 3:28). And Nephi emphasized, "He inviteth them all to come unto him and partake of his goodness; and he denieth none that come unto him, black and white, bond and free, male and female" (2 Nephi 26:33).

Elder David A. Bednar warned, "We may falsely think that such blessings and gifts are reserved for other people who appear to be more righteous or who serve in visible Church callings." He further emphasized: "To be or to become chosen is not an exclusive status conferred upon us. Rather, *you and I ultimately determine if we are chosen.*" He continued:

> Please now note the use of the word *chosen* in the following verses from the Doctrine and Covenants: "Behold, there are many called, but few are *chosen*. And why are they not *chosen*? Because their hearts are set so much upon the things of this world, and aspire to the honors of men" (D&C 121:34–35). I believe the implication

of these verses is quite straightforward. God does not have a list of favorites to which we must hope our names will someday be added. He does not limit "the chosen" to a restricted few. Rather, it is our hearts and *our* aspirations and *our* obedience which definitively determine whether we are counted as one of God's chosen.[2]

Heavenly Father wants to save every one of His children, but as Elder Bednar taught, it is not up to Him alone, for we do our own choosing in the way we keep or don't keep our covenants. Our quest during mortality is not to *become* chosen but to *remain* chosen, for as Peter learned, "God is no respecter of persons: But in every nation he that feareth him, and worketh righteousness, is accepted with him" (Acts 10:24–35). When God said, "Behold, this is my work and my glory—to bring to pass the immortality and eternal life of man" (Moses 1:39), He was referring to *all* of His children—not to some elected few who out-achieve everyone else.

At the last day God will choose and accept every person who has not refused to come. In other words, those who are un-chosen at the last day will only be those who have chosen to disqualify themselves from remaining chosen by refusing to repent. "But remember, God is merciful; therefore, repent of that which thou hast done which is contrary to the commandment which I gave you, and thou art still chosen" (D&C 3:10).

Bishop Richard C. Edgley, first counselor in the Presiding Bishopric, also spoke of the default situation as being chosen unless we un-choose ourselves. He first quoted the same scripture used by Elder Bednar: "Behold, there are many called, but few are chosen. And why are they not chosen? Because their hearts are set so much upon the things of this world, and aspire to the honors of men" (D&C 121:34–35). Then he said, "I believe the Lord is saying here that He calls, but we decide if we are chosen. Every member of the Church has been baptized, and thus, in a very real sense, we have all been called. We have been called to make and keep covenants. We have been called to be children of righteousness. *But we ourselves determine if we will be one of the chosen. We choose.*"[3]

Paul taught about our having been chosen during our premortal life when he said: "God hath from the beginning chosen you to salvation through sanctification of the Spirit and belief of the truth" (2 Thessalonians 2:13), and "According as he hath chosen us in him before the foundation of the world, that we should be holy and without blame before him in love" (Ephesians 1:4).

Even though we were all chosen in the premortal world, to remain chosen, there is still much work to be done during our mortal probation. There are covenants to make and keep as we learn to pattern our life after the Savior's example. As Nephi said, "Unless a man shall endure to the end, in following the example of the Son of the living God, he cannot be saved" (2 Nephi 31:16). He then added that if we desire to overcome our fallen nature and qualify to remain chosen at the last day, we must also "press forward with a steadfastness in Christ, having a perfect brightness of hope, and a love of God and of all men" (2 Nephi 31:20).

In this book we are going to learn how to attain that "perfect brightness of hope" that will give us the spiritual stamina to keep pressing forward in spite of all failures and opposition. We will learn how to correct our course when our "steadfastness in Christ" falters. We will gain a greater love for God, our fellow man, and ourselves. And most important, we will increase our faith and confidence in these beautiful and attainable promises of our Savior, that "blessed are they who are faithful and endure . . . for *they shall inherit eternal life*" (D&C 50:5; emphasis added). And: "Behold, mine arm of mercy is extended towards you, and *whosoever will come, him will I receive*; and blessed are those who come unto me" (3 Nephi 9:14; emphasis added). It is my testimony that these promises are within the reach of every living person who chooses to remain chosen and does not defeat themselves with doubt and fear.

I have chosen to explore these principles through an imaginary missionary who, because of past sins, feels un-chosen and perhaps even un-choosable. He is counseled and taught by an imaginary mission president. This fictional account will enable you to vicariously experience the remarkable process of repentance and second birth. It will guide you in learning the true meaning of godly sorrow and will assist you in building a firm and realistic expectation of being accepted and chosen to be with the Father for eternity. That is His plan for each of us unless we choose to decline the invitation.

Nothing that happens between our imaginary president and missionary in this fictional account is intended to reflect or represent official Church policy. Additionally, it would probably be unrealistic to expect a mission president to devote so much time or to teach a missionary in the depth of doctrine that this story presents. For the sake of our presentation, the doctrinal content has been expanded to cover our subjects and time has been condensed and accelerated.

Writing this book has increased the hope within me that I can and will be chosen. I hope it will do that for you as well.

—Steven A. Cramer

Notes

1 *Are We There Yet?*, 7; emphasis added.

2 "The Tender Mercies of the Lord," *Ensign*, May 2005, 101; emphasis added.

3 "Lessons from the Old Testament: Called of God," *Ensign*, Jan. 2006, 49; emphasis added.

The Rescue Begins

*P*resident Love was sitting in his office in the mission home, preparing for a busy day, when the doorbell rang. The mission home and offices were all combined into one building, with offices on the street level and living quarters on the upper floors. His wife was upstairs with the children, but he didn't go to the door because he knew his secretary would.

They had just reviewed the day's schedule, so he knew the unexpected caller was not a scheduled appointment, but he wasn't upset. As they'd gone over the list of things to be done, he'd felt a slight uneasiness, as though something might be missing from his plans. It was nothing he could put his finger on, but he'd sort of expected something unplanned to come up today. It was that gentle, kindly whispering of the Spirit on which he had come to rely.

He remembered how fearful he and his wife had been when they began this mission assignment, wondering how they could ever care for a hundred and fifty missionaries, let alone all the districts and branches he would be involved with. He smiled as he realized how foolish that fear had been. He'd felt the Spirit with him, guiding him and prompting him, teaching him the right things to say and do from the

1

very beginning. And so he waited expectantly, knowing that whatever situation was at the door would not be a problem he couldn't handle.

President Love was an ordinary looking man. He had brown, wavy hair touched with gray, and piercing eyes. To meet him for the first time would leave no particular impression if you were to judge by appearance alone. But you didn't have to be around him very long to feel the strength of his character. This was a man who loved God. You quickly felt his love for the work and for the people. And when it was time to leave him, you left feeling just a little lonely.

His secretary, Sister Richardson, soon appeared at his door with that same distressed look that she always had when she knew that their carefully planned agenda was about to be upset. She was a round woman, one you might imagine as an innkeeper's wife in a Charles Dickens movie. She had a warm and motherly nature that completely overshadowed her shape. With a constant smile and twinkle in her eye, the missionaries adored her, and she didn't mind it a bit. She loved to befriend the many young people who were here sacrificing to serve the Lord. Along with her husband, who managed the mission's fleet of vehicles, this senior couple was invaluable to the running of the mission.

"Who is it?" President Love asked.

"It's Elder Jones and Elder Curtis—and I don't think it's good."

"Why do you say that?"

"Well you know how happy and jovial Elder Jones is? Well, today he looks worried. And Elder Curtis didn't say anything; he just hung back, all nervous and fidgety. I told them your day was already scheduled and asked them if this wasn't something that could wait till the regular interviews at zone conference. But that seemed to make them even more nervous."

"Oh, Sister Richardson," he chided, frowning.

She hastily interrupted. "I know, I know, so I told them I'd talk to you and we'd figure out an appointment sometime in the next couple of days."

"Well, before we do that, why don't you have Elder Jones come in for a moment and let's see what this is about."

"But, President, what about the schedule we just agreed to?"

"Yes, yes, I know, Sister Richardson, but . . ."

"But people are always more important than schedules," she finished for him. "How many times you have told me!"

Knowing there was no changing his mind, she sighed and went to get Elder Jones. The president drove her crazy because he was always putting people ahead of their list of things to do. But she had learned a long time ago that, as hard as this made her job, it was also what made her admire him so much. And when you thought about it, that's the way the Savior was. The New Testament stories of His life are basically what happened as He responded to one interruption after another. She wondered if He ever got to do what He set out to do each day. It certainly didn't happen around here very often.

"Good morning, Elder Jones," said the president. "It's always good to see you. Please, sit down and tell me why you are here instead of out working."

Elder Jones was a tall, thin stick of a lad, like a runner whose flesh had been reduced to the minimum. He'd been a zone leader for about a year. He was one of the most dependable elders in the mission and was an easy person to love.

"President," he began, "its, well it's . . ." he faltered. "I can't really explain it, but there's something bothering Elder Curtis, and I can't get him to talk about it."

"Is it a problem between the two of you?" the president inquired, leaning forward.

"No, it's nothing like that. We get along great. But the last few weeks he's been really gloomy and just kind of going through the motions. I mean, don't get me wrong, he gets up on time and does everything he's supposed to do. In fact, he even gets up early. Way early. And he studies more than any companion I've ever had."

The president suggested, "Sometimes people use study time as an escape from doing. Is he unwilling to go out and work?"

"Oh no. In fact it wears me out trying to keep up with him. He seems driven. He wants to leave early and never wants to come home on time. He seems to know the principles of all the discussions. He's always studying in the *Preach My Gospel* manual. He can give any part of any discussion without advance notice. He's memorized most of the discussion scriptures. You wouldn't believe how much he studies. President, he used to be one of the best companions I've ever had. But . . ."

"Yes?"

"Well, President, now, it's kind of like his body is here, doing everything he's supposed to do, you know, going through the motions, but his heart isn't in it anymore." He fell silent, struggling to find a better explanation. "President, I love Elder Curtis, and I've tried everything I know to cheer him up. But . . . well, I'm sorry, but I just don't know what more to do."

President Love gave him a moment to calm his feelings, thinking what a marvelous work and a wonder it is that the Lord trusts such responsibilities to these young men and women. "Thank you, Elder Jones. You did the right thing to come. I appreciate your feelings for your companion, and I know the Lord appreciates your desire to help him too. Why don't you go upstairs and wait in the living room while I speak with Elder Curtis. Would you please send him in?"

Elder Jones rose from the chair, eager to transfer the problem, much like a runner passing the baton after doing his lap of the relay. As he left, President Love said, "By the way, you'll find the new conference issue of the *Ensign* up there. You might enjoy reading that while I talk to your companion."

A moment later Elder Curtis knocked timidly on the office door.

"Elder Curtis, come in, come in and sit down." He said, "Thanks for coming to see me," as if the elder had done the president a favor by interrupting his plans. Elder Curtis was a handsome young man. He was short but well-built. He had wavy blond hair and blue eyes that drew your attention.

The president said, "Let's see, you've been with us for about six months now. Please, tell me how you are feeling about your mission since the last time we talked."

"Well, President, the mission part is going fine. We're busy and teaching lots of investigators and I should be happy . . ." His voice trailed off. "It's just . . ." He paused to gather strength. Then he rushed forward with, "Well, I've got a problem stuck in the way and I can't seem to get past it." His eyes dropped and his head lowered slowly as he said, "I'm sorry to let you down like this."

President Love moved his chair from behind his desk so that he could sit closer to the elder. He said tenderly, "Elder Curtis, you haven't let me down at all. I'm sorry that you have a problem, but I'm glad that you came to see me. Now that you're here, I hope you will trust me enough to share what it is that's bothering you."

He looked at the president in astonishment. What he had expected was some form of chastisement, along with a pep talk about being tough and enduring to the end instead of giving in to discouragement.

But the president didn't seem at all angry or even annoyed. In fact, it sounded like he might actually care about what was bothering him. This response confused him because he figured that if *he* were a busy leader, with lots of responsibilities and important things to do, he would most certainly be upset if one of his workers came into the office unannounced, whining about a problem instead of going out and doing his job.

"You're *glad* that I have a problem?" he stammered.

"Well, not exactly. But I'm glad that since you do have one, you've come to me with it. I've learned that my problems are my teachers, and that if I look upon them as opportunities instead of roadblocks, I benefit by learning the lessons they can teach me. And the sooner I do that, the sooner I'm able to move on. So why don't you level with me, Elder. Is it a companion problem?"

"Oh no, President. Elder Jones is a really good companion, and I try to do everything he asks."

"Well then, is it a family problem? Are you homesick?" He was about to continue with other suggestions that might help the elder open up when he was interrupted by a burst of emotion.

"No, it's nothing like that. It's . . ." Elder Curtis paused, mustering his courage. "Sir, I lied to my bishop and stake president about my worthiness, so I shouldn't be here. I'm not worthy to be a missionary, and you should send me home."

"I see," said the president thoughtfully. "Then you were certainly right to come and tell me. But, Elder Curtis, before we can decide whether you stay on your mission or have to go home, I'll need to hear the whole truth. You need to tell me what it is that you were not truthful about and what it is that makes you feel you are not worthy of this calling. Do you think you can do that now?"

Elder Curtis squirmed in his chair, hesitating, as if he had not yet made up his mind, but eventually he said, "Yes, President, I should have done this a long time ago. I'm ready if you are willing to help me."

President Love knew better than to expect the elder to jump right into the heart of the problem. One had to work up to that. So, after kneeling together in prayer, he invited Elder Curtis to sit down again and tell him how he felt about the gospel. Elder Curtis spoke with confidence as he expressed appreciation for his parents and family and for his membership in the Church. He bore testimony of the gospel and said that he had always known it was true. The president could feel the strength of his convictions.

But as Elder Curtis tried to say that he was thankful to be on a mission, he faltered and looked at President Love with eyes that betrayed his dread of saying what needed to be said next.

Offering a short reprieve, and before encouraging Elder Curtis's confession, he said, "Elder Curtis, we are about to enter upon a pivotal point in your life. You are distressed because you feel that you have been living a lie. Our Lord and Master taught us that only the truth could make us free. You say that you have been hiding the truth, but now you are ready to face it. That means that you are on the verge of growth. It means that the Savior and His angels are rejoicing because you are about to step out of your darkness into the light of honesty and truth.

"Of course they grieve with you for whatever sins have put you into this state, but they rejoice that God's loving gift of conscience has worked inside you to bring you to this point. Whatever your problem is, if you are ready to face it with honesty and with resolve to grow, then I know that the Savior is ready to take your hand and walk the path with you back to forgiveness and cleanliness. He has promised not that He waits for you at the end of that path but that He is the way back, meaning that no one need walk that path alone.

"Now tell me, what was it that happened before your mission that made you feel you needed to hide it from your bishop and stake president? Were you too much involved with a young woman?"

After a long pause, the elder cleared his throat and hung his head. He squirmed in his chair as he explained, "No, it wasn't *a* young woman; it was *hundreds* of them. In high school I got hooked on pornography. I knew it wasn't right, but somehow it seemed less evil than corrupting real girls. I know that sounds stupid now, but it seemed to make sense back then. Anyhow, I knew I couldn't serve a mission with that stuff floating around in my head, so I tried to quit. It took a long time and it wasn't easy, but I did repent. Before I put in my papers, I forced myself not to indulge for a full six months before my mission interviews. That seemed like a lifetime. I told myself that if I repented for that long, then it would be okay to tell my leaders that I was morally clean. But . . ." He trailed off into silence.

The president offered, "That was a remarkable achievement, but you still didn't feel clean, did you?"

"No, President, I didn't."

"That's because when we try to hide our sins, they rot and fester inside us. What was it that prevented you from confessing this to your leaders so that you could get rid of the burden?"

"I just couldn't. I knew they would say that I had to wait, or that perhaps I could never come on a mission. That would have devastated my parents. I wouldn't know how to face people. It would have been so embarrassing. People would look down on me if they knew how rotten I was inside. I just couldn't face all that."

He looked up, hoping the president would approve of his thinking. He explained, "I thought I could make it right by coming here and serving valiantly and I've tried hard to do that. During the six months I've been here, I've read the Book of Mormon twice and almost all of the New Testament. I've also read *A Marvelous Work and a Wonder*, and even *Jesus the Christ* by Talmage. I've memorized almost all of the discussion scriptures and I've studied the entire *Preach My Gospel* manual twice." Suddenly he realized how boastful that all sounded, so he added, "I thought if I was a really good missionary, maybe that would, well, you know, kind of even things out, and then I could be okay with the Lord."

"Elder, I think that Satan tricks a lot of people into believing that they can avoid justice by trying to compensate or trade some good works for their sins." Elder Curtis blushed. "I'm sure they don't think of it this way, but what that deception does is invite us to concoct our own substitute plan for the Savior's Atonement."

The elder rose halfway up from his chair and started to protest that he never meant it that way, but the president waved him quiet.

"Elder Curtis, those were good things to do to become a better missionary, but all your good works for the rest of your life could never pay for your sins or make you feel clean. I can see that you've put in a lot of extra work. And while I appreciate your efforts, don't think you can impress the Lord with a checklist of good deeds. Look, you attended seminary; you heard all the lessons on repentance. So let's think about it together: did you actually repent, or did you just stop doing the sin? And why do *you* think it didn't work?"

Elder Curtis didn't speak for a long time. The president waited, knowing he needed to chew on it awhile. His body shook as he speculated softly: "Because real repentance is more than just stopping doing something wrong."

"That's true," said the president. "If stopping is as far as we go, it is like cutting off the tops of the weeds in our garden. Unless we dig them out by the roots, they are going to grow right back and eventually they will choke out our vegetables. But what else was wrong?"

Elder Curtis sighed and his shoulders slumped. "Part of repentance is to be really sorry for your sins. Even though I did stop for six months, I wasn't really sorry for the lust and fantasies. I was just afraid I was going to get found out. To be truthful, I missed it, and I was wishing all that time that I could go back to it."

"Thank you for admitting that, but what else was missing?"

The elder was almost angry. "Isn't that enough? What more do you want from me?"

The president replied, "Elder, we're not talking about what *I* want from you but what the *Lord* needs from you before He can apply His Atonement and help you find His cleansing forgiveness and peace. Here, I know you've heard this before, but let's read the Lord's test of sincere repentance. It's right here in D&C 58:43. You read it aloud, Elder."

The elder took the president's worn scriptures and read: " 'By this ye may know if a man repenteth of his sins—behold, he will confess them and forsake them.' " He looked pretty discouraged.

"So besides hiding the truth and not really feeling remorse, what else was missing, Elder?"

"Okay, real repentance means you don't hide your sin or pretend that it's okay because you are not doing it anymore. You have to confess it, to face up to it, to come clean and not hide it inside. Look, I hate having it inside. It just keeps eating at me. It keeps growing and growing. President, I haven't looked at pornography or masturbated for over a year now. I'm here serving the Lord. I work extra hard. I've even baptized some people. So why does this monster of guilt keep getting bigger and bigger until it is taking over my life? It doesn't seem fair," he protested angrily, as if someone had wronged him.

President Love watched him for a moment and then said sternly, "Elder, what you have been feeling is not only *fair*, but it is a gift of divine love. Once you come to understand how the Lord deals with these things, you will actually be grateful for the pain that He gives in consequence of our sins."

"I doubt that," lamented the elder. "No one could be grateful to feel as I do."

The president did not reply for a while. He just stared at the boy, thinking how grateful he was for the divine gift of conscience, which the Lord so lovingly placed within each of us so that we could never comfortably hide or indulge secret sins.

"Elder Curtis," he said, clasping the elder's hand and pulling him out of his chair, "thank you for telling me the truth. I admire you for having the courage to do that. I wish you could have done this before your mission because that would have spared you much heartache." He tried to hug the elder, but Elder Curtis stiffened and pulled away. The president was disappointed, but it told him what he needed to know.

"So, how long before you send me home?"

He said, "Elder, what you did was very wrong, but it is not the end of the world. Before we can decide about staying here or going home, I'm going to help you untangle this mistake. We'll talk it through, and when we get it sorted out, then we'll decide what needs to be done."

The elder felt confused. He asked, "What do you mean untangle?"

The president explained, "You and I are going to review some of the principles that you were taught in seminary, Sunday school, and, I'm sure, by your parents as well. We are going to take a look at the kind and loving plan the Lord has given to His children to help us get out of these terrible holes that we dig ourselves into. In between our sessions, I am going to have you study some articles that I've written.

"Normally that would take us several weeks of interviews, but because of your situation, I don't think we should drag things out that long. I'm going to have you stay here in the mission home for the next couple of days so that we can get this taken care of. Elder Brown is in the hospital having some minor knee surgery. We expect him back next week, but in the meanwhile, that leaves an opening here in the office staff that I've been wondering how to fill. I'm going to temporarily assign you to take his place.

"Sister Richardson thinks things are quite busy around here, but actually, all that I really need to focus on for the next few days is preparing for zone conferences. That means I'll be here in the office most of the time anyway. And since most of Elder Brown's work can wait until he gets back, that will give us lots of opportunities to meet together and talk without drawing attention to you.

"We are going to use this opportunity to learn how kind your Father in Heaven and your Savior are. After you come to understand these things, then we'll decide what to do about your situation.

"As you know, the next floor up is filled with bunk beds for the elders or sisters who are arriving or leaving the mission. You can sleep there and have your meals with our family."

This was a totally unexpected turn of events. "But, but . . ." he stammered, "what about Elder Jones? And what about all our appointments?"

"You don't need to worry about any of that. I'll assign him to work with Elder Johnson and Elder Rich. He was already scheduled to give them some training next week, so we'll just move that up a week. Besides, you've already told me that you don't feel worthy to represent the Lord."

Somewhat defiantly, Elder Curtis backed away a bit and retorted defensively, "Well, I admit I'm not perfect, but Elder Jones and I have baptized five people in the last three months."

"And what does that have to do with being worthy?" asked the president, somewhat annoyed at this show of false pride. "Sit down. You say that you've studied the *Preach My Gospel* manual. You tell me, what does it say is the main stewardship responsibility of the missionaries? Is it to baptize people into the Church?"

"Well, of course it is. Everybody knows that's why we go out every day, to convert people to the gospel and baptize them."

"No, Elder, that is not it at all." He opened the manual to page one. "Here, let's read it together. You see the title: 'What Is My Purpose as a Missionary' and then the very first statement: 'Invite others to come unto Christ.' Let's turn to page two. I want you to read these two sentences that I have highlighted."

The elder read: " 'You are called to represent Jesus Christ in helping people become clean from their sins. You do this by inviting them to come unto Jesus Christ and become converted to His restored gospel.' "

The president took back the manual and then turned so that they were face to face. "How can you possibly introduce someone to a Savior that you don't even know because you yourself are unclean and unforgiven? How can you think to bring your investigators to someone that you don't even trust? Someone that you have tried to shortcut around?" He handed his Doctrine and Covenants to the elder again. "Here, I want you to read what the Lord said to the Prophet Joseph's brother, Hyrum."

The elder took the book and read: " 'Behold, this is your work, to keep my commandments, yea, with all your might, mind and strength. Seek not to declare my word, *but first seek to obtain my word*, and then shall your tongue be loosed; then, if you desire, you shall have my Spirit and my word, yea, the power of God unto the convincing of men' (D&C 11:20–21; emphasis added)."

The president observed, "I suspect that Hyrum was just as clean and worthy as Joseph was, and yet the Lord asked him to learn His gospel before he tried to share it with others."

The elder protested, "But our converts *did* get baptized. And I know they believe."

"So you gave them a good introduction to the Church. But your job was to bring them to Christ. Hopefully, as they attend and continue to learn, someone will teach them about Christ and the way back to Him, but you have got some learning and some repenting to do before you can fulfill that stewardship. You may have read and memorized a lot of things, but you certainly haven't 'obtained' or understood that part of the word of Christ that changes lives and brings peace. Now what do you say, are you ready to start?"

Elder Curtis mumbled a yes while the president opened a file drawer, thumbed through some well-worn folder tabs, and pulled out a paper entitled: "The Conscience—a Gift of Love." Handing it to the elder, the president said: "I see that you have your backpack with you. Does that mean you have your own scriptures?"

"Yes, of course."

"Good, then I want you to study this discussion on the conscience. Feel free to mark it up or put ideas in the margins because it is yours to keep. You asked me why the monster of guilt keeps growing and gnawing at you when you are no longer continuing in sin. What you have been experiencing is one of the most powerful and loving gifts that Heavenly Father has given to help us recognize good from evil— and to protect us from continuing in sin when we make wrong choices. After you have studied this, we'll talk together again."

Then, pausing as if he'd just thought of something else that could help, he reflected, "Actually, Elder, our conscience works something like a Geiger counter. Do you know what that is?"

"Yeah. It's an instrument that measures radiation, isn't it?"

"That's right, but so does a dosimeter. I'd like you to think about the difference and decide which one is most like the conscience."

"I think I've heard of dosimeters, but I'm not sure what they do."

"Well, you can almost guess by the name. They measure the dose, or accumulated amount of radiation that an individual person has received. They function silently. On the other hand, Geiger counters measure the amount of radiation present in a specific area. And they are very noisy. The clicks they make are in proportion to the amount or strength of the radiation particles they detect. The more radiation there is, the louder they click. So, Elder, which instrument do you think best compares to the conscience?"

Elder Curtis actually grinned. "What you are saying is that my Geiger-counter conscience has been sensing more and more guilt and so it is screaming at me louder and louder. Is that it?" he asked.

The president did not answer directly. Instead, he stood and put his hand on the elder's shoulder as he said, "Let's see if you can find the answer as you study this article. Then you come back and explain it to me. Okay?"

Elder Curtis was totally baffled by why he wasn't already on the way to the airport. He was not sure what the president was up to. He just sat there, uncertain what was expected of him. The president, however, knew exactly what he was doing. He had been through similar discussions with other missionaries, and he knew what it would take to open this elder's heart to the simple majesty of the gift of repentance.

He knew the Lord would not want any missionary to go home if it could be prevented, but that decision would be made later, by inspiration and in consultation with the Missionary Department in Salt Lake City. In the meanwhile, the charge that he had received in his setting apart to nurture and care for the missionaries made him determined to do all that he could to teach the elder and help the Lord rescue a lost sheep.

He pulled the elder out of his chair again. Let's go explain this to Elder Jones. You'll both need to go to your apartment and get the clothes and other things you'll need for two or three days. By the time you get back, I'll have Elder Johnson and Elder Rich here for Elder Jones.

"When you get back, you go see Sister Richardson and she'll show you where Elder Brown's cubicle is. You can study there or you can go upstairs to the living room, whichever you prefer. After you've studied the article on the conscience, then come on back here to my office and we'll talk some more."

President Love went upstairs to let his wife know that there would be an extra mouth to feed for the next couple of days because Elder Curtis would be staying with them. His wife looked tired, but beautiful as always. She was dressing the children for school. The moment she saw that familiar look on his face, she knew he was concerned about something important. Sometimes she worried that he took too much burden upon himself. She stood and put her arms around him as she smiled and teased playfully, "So, you're at it again, aren't you, honey?"

He immediately sensed that she wanted to lighten things up. It was her way of sustaining him in the work he took so seriously, and he knew that sometimes he did need to lighten up a bit. So, pretending not to have a clue, he smiled and replied, "Now, whatever are you talking about?"

They had played this game before, and the words came almost by rote. He knew that she loved the missionaries and worried over them as much as he did. It was just her way of trying to help him, and he loved her for it.

"Don't be coy with me, big boy! You know exactly what I'm talking about," she said with a twinkle in her eye. "I know why there's an extra mouth to feed. It's one of those leaving-the-ninety-and-nine opportunities that you like so much."

She continued with an exaggerated, accusatory voice: "I'll bet you are going to drop your regular duties so that you can spend all your time working with one troubled soul, aren't you?" as if her accusation had indicted him of some terrible deed. He knew, however, that she was only recognizing and honoring his faithfulness to his stewardship.

"No, I'm not dropping any of my duties," he replied, pretending to be defensive, but staying true to the game. "This 'working on one soul,' as you say, is a huge challenge, but an important part of any mission president's life. You well know that we have as much stewardship toward the missionaries as we do to the investigators—if not more. Besides," he said, returning the playful accusation, "You know you would do the same thing if you had the chance!" She just smiled, knowing the game was over.

Then, sobering, he said more seriously, "Sweetheart, it's important for this elder to learn how the Atonement takes place one person at a time—and that it is past time for his turn."

She gave him a parting hug as she whispered lovingly, "I know dear, and you are just the one to teach him that. I'll be praying for you both."

As he turned and headed back down the stairs, he was already engaged in his own prayerful petition for the guidance and insight he would need to help this elder.

The Conscience—A Gift of Love

After obtaining their things from the apartment, the two elders returned to the mission home. They found Elders Johnson and Rich waiting for them. Elder Jones left with them, and Elder Curtis put his things upstairs on one of the bunk beds. Sister Richardson got him settled in Elder Brown's cubicle and left him to his studies. With Elder Brown's companion assigned to the field for a few days, he felt comfortable and private after realizing there wasn't anyone else working in the office but Elder and Sister Richardson.

He had fully expected to be at the airport by now. After pondering the unexpected turn of events and failing to determine what it was going to mean for his future, he resigned himself to his assignment. He said a quick prayer, more out of habit than sincerity. He settled in at the desk and began to read.

The Conscience—A Gift of Love

We don't like the pain we feel when we burn ourselves, but that pain is a gift from God that prompts us to pull back from the heat, thereby protecting our flesh from further harm. Imagine the damage if we didn't have that instant sensory warning of physical danger.

Similarly, we don't enjoy the guilty feelings roused by our conscience when we do something wrong. But that spiritual pain, which is inflicted by our conscience, is also a gift from God that is intended to alert us to spiritual danger and to encourage us to pull back from choices that are leading us down the wrong path. As Elder Boyd K. Packer explained, "You have an alarm system built into both body and spirit. In your body it is pain; in your spirit it is guilt—or spiritual pain. While neither pain nor guilt is pleasant, and an excess of either can be destructive, both are a protection, for they sound the alarm 'Don't do that again!' " ("To Young Women and Men," *Ensign*, May 1989, 54, 59).

Think about the spiritual damage to our lives if we didn't have warnings from our conscience and continued in sin until it became addictive and destroyed us. How grateful we should be for our "annoying" consciences and the "just law given, which [brings] remorse of conscience unto man" when he sins (see Alma 42:15–19). As Elder Packer emphasized, "Be grateful for both. If the nerve endings in your hands were altered so that you couldn't feel pain, you might put them in fire or machinery and destroy them. In your teenage heart of hearts, you know right from wrong (see 2 Nephi 2:5). Learn to pay attention to that spiritual voice of warning within you" ("To Young Women and Men," *Ensign*, May 1989, 59).

Everyone Starts with a Conscience

Elder Richard G. Scott gave the assurance that "every individual born to earth is given a detecting capability, a divinely appointed gift to distinguish truth from error. We call it our conscience. God calls it the Spirit of Christ. When we properly use this gift, we are naturally drawn to truth and repelled from error" ("Happiness Now and Forever," *Ensign*, Nov. 1979, 70).

We see this verified in scripture. For example, "And the Spirit giveth light to every man that cometh into the world; and the Spirit enlighteneth every man through the world, that hearkeneth to the voice of the Spirit" (D&C 84:46), and "I am the true light that lighteth every man that cometh into the world" (D&C 93:2). Thus, Mormon declared boldly, "My brethren, it is given unto you to judge, that ye may know good from evil; and the way to judge is as plain, that ye may know with a perfect knowledge, as the daylight is from the dark night. For behold, the Spirit of Christ is given to every man, that he may know good from evil" (Moroni 7:15–16). And so it was that Bruce R. McConkie wrote:

Every person born into the world is endowed with the light of Christ as a free gift (D&C 84:45–48). By virtue of this endowment all men automatically and intuitively know right from wrong and are encouraged and enticed to do what is right (Moroni 7:16). The recognizable operation of this Spirit in enlightening the mind and striving to lead men to do right is called conscience. It is an inborn consciousness or sense of the moral goodness or blameworthiness of one's conduct, intentions, and character, together with an instinctive feeling or obligation to do right or be good (*Mormon Doctrine*, 156–157; emphasis added).

The Conscience Is Positive

Some people mistakenly interpret the proddings of their conscience as a form of punishment, but this is not true. It is not something negative that is meant to pull us down; it should be positive and lifting and encouraging. Elder Neal A. Maxwell pointed out that "when conscience calls to us from the next ridge, it is not solely to *scold* but also to *beckon*" ("Notwithstanding My Weakness," *Ensign*, Nov. 1976, 14; emphasis added). The Lord loves us too much to simply stand idly by and watch us succumb to temptation without inviting us to turn from our fallen nature. We should welcome those nudges from our conscience because they are not only *warnings*, but also divine *invitations*, for "whom I love I also chasten that their sins may be forgiven, for with the chastisement I prepare a way for their deliverance in all things out of temptation, and I have loved you" (D&C 95:1).

Once, while camping, I found myself visited by a tiny chipmunk. He was scurrying all about my camp as though expecting—probably based on experience—to receive free nourishment. I was happy to share and tossed a cracker near where he posed, statue-like. But he ignored my offered gift and quickly dashed to another spot. Eager to share, I tossed another cracker to that spot, but in his preoccupation with scurrying, he didn't notice this one either. This continued through several more attempts until I despaired of sharing with him. I suspect that he may have ignored the crackers because he interpreted them as threats rather than gifts.

Sometime later that day, I noticed that he had finally discovered one of the crackers. He held it in his two little paws and nibbled in obvious delight at finding this new treasure. It made me feel good to have blessed his life in this way. As I considered this experience, I was reminded of the Lord's disclosure: "And how great is his joy in the soul that repenteth" (D&C 18:13). And I wondered, "When the Lord sends promptings to me through my conscience (only to

be ignored as I scurry busily about my life), does He feel frustration like I felt when I couldn't persuade the chipmunk that I was his
friend and was trying to help him?"

At this point, Elder Curtis paused and thought, *So that's why the
president said it was a good thing this is happening to me. Instead of feeling
terrible, I should value the warning and do whatever it takes to make the
pain go away. I can see now that if I respond to my conscience immediately,
instead of ignoring it or trying to smother it with good works and hoping it
will go away, it will help me to be happy. It is not something to be resented but,
rather, appreciated as a gift from Heavenly Father.* Then his eye moved to
the subtitle of the next section and he resumed reading, now anxious
for new understanding.

What Happens When We Ignore Our Conscience

The power of an ignored conscience can vary all the way from
mild irritation, such as "he shall not feel quietness in his belly," (Job
20:20) to the terror felt by Alma, which he described as being so
terrible that "the very thought of coming into the presence of my
God did *rack my soul with inexpressible horror*" (Alma 36:14; emphasis
added). When we choose to ignore the conscience's warning signals,
they can turn into a relentless, gnawing mental anguish. Zeezrom
felt such anguish because of his persecution of Alma and Amulek,
which sins "did harrow up his mind until it did become exceedingly
sore, *having no deliverance*; therefore he began to be scorched with
a burning heat" and "*his mind . . . was exceedingly sore because of his
iniquities*" (Alma 15:3, 5; emphasis added).

Elder Curtis thought: *Yes, that is exactly what's been happening to me!*
He thought he remembered that Zeezrom had later repented and joined
the Church. Excitedly he looked up the name of Zeezrom in the index
in the back of his triple combination scriptures and was delighted to
verify that not only was that true but that he also went with Alma and
Amulek on their mission to the Zoramites, and his teachings were even
quoted later by the prophet Helaman. He thought, *If the Lord could forgive and accept Zeezrom, who almost got the prophet Alma killed, surely there
is a chance that He could forgive and accept me too.* He continued reading.

The conscience is a very delicate instrument of the spirit mind
and if we abuse it by prolonged neglect, as we persist in deliberate evil,

we can destroy it. The scriptures speak of those whose deliberately prolonged sin has caused them to degenerate spiritually until they "are past feeling," or have "their conscience seared with a hot iron" until "even their mind and conscience is defiled" (see Ephesians 4:19; 1 Nephi 17:45; Moroni 9:20; 1 Timothy 4:2; Titus 1:15). Thus the Lord warned of the shutting down of the conscience: "And he that repents not, from him shall be taken even the light which he has received; for my Spirit shall not always strive with man, saith the Lord of Hosts" (D&C 1:33).

Elder Spencer W. Kimball echoed that warning when he noted that "a man may rationalize and excuse himself till the groove is so deep he cannot get out without great difficulty" (*The Miracle of Forgiveness*, 86). Similarly, King Benjamin warned: "I say unto you, my brethren, that after ye have known and have been taught all these things, if ye should transgress and go contrary to that which has been spoken, that ye do withdraw yourselves from the Spirit of the Lord, that it may have no place in you to guide you in wisdom's paths that ye may be blessed, prospered, and preserved" (Mosiah 2:36). The final consequence to those who destroy their conscience and refuse to repent is that they "are consigned to an awful view of their own guilt and abominations, which doth cause them to shrink from the presence of the Lord into a state of misery and endless torment, from whence they can no more return; therefore they have drunk damnation to their own souls" (Mosiah 3:25).

Paul wrote a cryptic warning about this when he said: "Quench not the Spirit" (1 Thessalonians 5:19). The Greek translation renders this warning as to not extinguish, hinder, or suppress the Spirit—as we do when we ignore the conscience. The Book of Mormon explains Paul's warning in greater detail: "Behold, will ye reject these words? Will ye reject the words of the prophets; and will ye reject all the words which have been spoken concerning Christ, after so many have spoken concerning him; and deny the good word of Christ, and the power of God, and the gift of the Holy Ghost, and quench the Holy Spirit, and make a mock of the great plan of redemption, which hath been laid for you?" (Jacob 6:8).

On the other hand, honoring our conscience brings the spiritual gifts of peace and confidence before God. When King Benjamin's people repented and committed their lives to Christ, they not only "received a remission of their sins" but also a *"peace of conscience*, because of their exceeding faith which they had in Jesus Christ" (Mosiah 4:3; emphasis added). As we seek to perfect ourselves, we should strive to join Paul who reflected: "I have lived in all good conscience before God until this day" and "herein do I exercise myself, to have always a conscience void of offence toward God, and toward men" (Acts 23:1; 24:16). Similarly, Job vowed: "My righteousness I hold fast, and will not let it go: my heart shall not reproach me so long as I live" (Job 27:6), and King Benjamin indicated that he had spent his life "walking with a clear conscience before God" and that "I can answer a clear conscience before God this day" (Mosiah 2:27, 15). We know this is possible for us as well because the Lord has not only advised us to "let virtue garnish thy thoughts unceasingly" but has promised that as we do so, "then shall thy confidence wax strong in the presence of God" (D&C 121:45). Thus, when our thoughts and conscience are clear, we can say, at any time and without hesitation, "Search me, O God, and know my heart: try me, and know my thoughts," for "happy is he that condemneth not himself in that thing which he alloweth" (Psalm 139:23; Romans 14:22).

One of the great motivators for repenting is the knowledge that the joy that comes from responding to a wounded conscience is often proportional to the pain we felt before our repentance. For example, Alma stated that after his repentance and surrender to Christ, "I could remember my pains no more; yea, I was harrowed up by the memory of my sins no more. And oh, what joy, and what marvelous light I did behold; yea my soul was filled with joy as exceeding as was my pain! Yea, I say unto you, my son, that there could be nothing so exquisite and so bitter as were my pains. Yea, and again I say unto you, my son, that on the other hand, there can be nothing so exquisite and sweet as was my joy" (Alma 36:19–21). And John taught: "Beloved, if our heart condemn us not, then have we confidence toward God (1 John 3:21).

Elder Curtis realized that he, even more than Joseph's brother, Hyrum, did indeed have a lot to learn in "obtaining" a true understanding of the gospel. Reverently he set down the paper and bowed his head. This time his prayer was more heartfelt. "Heavenly Father, I'm tired of living with an angry conscience. I'm grateful that you never gave up on me and allowed my conscience to continue working with me. I don't know what I have to do, but I promise that I will work and study and learn and repent until I can stand clean before Thee. Please help me to learn how."

Further Discussion on
the Conscience

*E*lder Curtis found Sister Richardson at her desk and asked what
he must do to see the president again. "You don't need appointments
for that anymore, Elder. His time belongs to you today. Just go on in
the office. He is waiting for you."

"You mean the *whole* day?" he asked incredulously. "What about
his schedule?"

"Elder, you have no idea how much the president loves you, do you?
You *are* his schedule for all of today—and tomorrow too if you need
it. He can fit his zone conference preparations in between your counseling sessions. You go on in there." As he turned to leave, she added,
"And, elder, do try to believe what he tells you."

He knocked on the door with a bit more confidence. The president's warm greeting made him feel as if he were someone important
instead of an elder about to be sent home.

As soon as he was seated, the President said, "All right, Elder, let's
get on with it. Why don't we start by you telling me something you
learned from your study."

He replied, "I learned a lot. I never knew the conscience was such
an important part of getting us back to Heavenly Father. If the warning

light started flashing red in my car or the smoke alarm started buzzing in our house, I wouldn't ignore those. I would respond immediately, or else I might ruin the engine or die in a fire. So now I can see how stupid it is to ignore my conscience because those warnings are even more important. I also learned how lucky I am that my conscience hasn't shut down and the Holy Ghost hasn't stopped working on me."

"It wasn't luck, Elder," the president corrected. "It was God's love. He never *wants* to withdraw His help from us. It is only when we deliberately and intentionally rebel over long periods of time, without even wanting or trying to repent, that we may damage our conscience sufficiently to drive the Spirit reluctantly away from us." He smiled as he said, "You didn't force your conscience to shut down because you did forsake the sin, and that shows integrity."

Elder Curtis showed him the paper he had been studying. "I marked it here, where Elder Maxwell explained that the guilty feelings we have from our conscience are not just to scold us but also to beckon us. That surprised me. I thought I was being punished because I didn't confess the full truth, but this almost makes it sound like these feelings of guilt are not to punish me for doing wrong and being dishonest but to invite me to repent and come closer to Christ. Is that right?"

"Elder, Christ is always and forever reaching out to us and inviting us to come to Him. I am so glad you were touched by that insight. The scriptures contain over six hundred revelations on repentance. It is time to reintroduce you to one of the most important repentance scriptures the Lord has given us. Open your Bible and let's turn to 2 Corinthians and read what Paul said to some people that he had previously challenged to repent."

Elder Curtis read: " 'Now I rejoice, not that ye were made sorry, but that ye sorrowed to repentance: for ye were made sorry after a godly manner, that ye might receive damage by us in nothing. For godly sorrow worketh repentance to salvation not to be repented of: but the sorrow of the world worketh death' (2 Corinthians 7:9–10)."

"Elder, what do we learn from these two verses?"

"Well, Paul talks about there being two kinds of sorrow that people who need to repent might feel, but I'd never thought about it this way. I just always thought that guilt was guilt."

"But where did he mention guilt?" asked the president.

"Well, he didn't, but doesn't sorrow mean the same thing? Somebody sins and their conscience makes them feel guilty so they are sorry they sinned."

The president explained, "Paul is teaching about something a lot more divine and inviting than guilt. The guilt you mentioned is what he meant by worldly sorrow, which can be described as guilty feelings of shame that make us hate ourselves and feel worthless when we know we've done wrong but are not willing to repent and change. Godly sorrow, on the other hand, is something much more divine. It is more like feeling remorse that we have done something to disappoint our Heavenly Father and thereby withdrawn ourselves from Him. Godly sorrow lifts us. It entices us to repent and do all we can to get right again with God. It is that beckoning invitation that Elder Maxwell was talking about.

"I remind you that the war which began in the premortal world has never ended. That war continues here in mortality. The two great powers at war on this earth are both fighting for the souls of men. You know that one is Christ, who will lead us back to the Father. The other is Satan, with all who follow him, who are working feverishly to deceive and prevent us from returning to the Father."

He continued, "Heavenly Father's goal, and the Savior's goal, is to promote our victory over our fallen natures and lead us to happiness and joy. Satan's goal is to promote our misery and captivity. And so we come to Paul's insights about the conscience. Heavenly Father gives a conscience to every person to alert them to spiritual danger, like that warning light you mentioned or the smoke alarm. Our conscience warns us with feelings of sorrow that teach us that we just made a mistake. And if we are responsive and willing to repent, those feelings lift us and motivate us to accept the Savior's invitation to come to Him in sincere repentance.

"But Satan does not want that to happen. So he instantly attacks, suggesting to our minds the feelings of horrible guilt and self-deprecating shame that usually stop us from praying or moving forward. This is the worldly sorrow that pulls us downward, away from God, and chains us to our past. I'm going to give you some materials to study more about this. But first I want you to read some quotations from the prophets. You might even want to keep this in your copy of *Preach My Gospel.* Or you could fold it and keep it in your scriptures."

Elder Curtis took the paper and read aloud, " 'Before the many elements of repentance are set in motion, there has to be a first step. That first step is the turning point at which the sinner consciously recognizes his sin. This is the awakening, the conviction of guilt.' "[1] The next quotation added, " 'When we come to recognize our sin sincerely and without reservations, we are ready to follow such processes as will rid us of sin's effects.' "[2]

"Elder, excuse me," interrupted the president. "Before you read Elder Maxwell, let me say something about that. President Kimball talked about a turning point where the sinner decides to change. You had the opportunity of that turning point when you contemplated putting in your mission papers. But instead of fully embracing the godly sorrow that your conscience was offering, as an invitation to rise above your fallen nature, you decided not to repent all the way.

"You recognized and abandoned your sin. That took a lot of courage and was a huge decision and accomplishment. It shows that you wanted to get right with the Lord. But, unfortunately, you allowed your fear to override the rest of your duty and decided to withhold the truth from your bishop and stake president. By making that mistake, you chose the worldly way of hiding your sin." He smiled at the miserable Elder and said, kindly, "I'm not reminding you of this to make you feel worse but to help you understand the Lord's process." He paused and got a book from the shelf. Post-it notes marked various pages. He browsed for a moment, found what he wanted, and said, "President Kimball once reported on having interviewed lots of people with situations very similar to yours. Let's have you read the warning he expressed to them."

Elder Curtis read, " '[Sin] is not something that can be set aside with a brushing-off gesture, or even with feigned sorrow, or even with a determination never to repeat the error.' "[3] He blushed.

Not in the least embarrassed or hesitant to firm this principle, the president added, "Over here, on the next page please," pointing to another highlight.

Reluctantly, the elder read, " 'If you committed murder and then merely felt a little sorry, would you feel that you should be permitted immediately all privileges of freedom you formerly possessed, merely because you intended never to repeat the act? Do you think you should pay no price? No penalty? No adjustment?' "[4] The president continued,

"Elder, you were tricked into thinking that you could shortcut your way around the divine system the Lord has established. Do you see how choosing worldly sorrow over godly sorrow allowed your shame to degenerate into the prolonged guilt that is tormenting you now?"

"Yes, President, I do. I didn't understand it then, or I would have chosen differently."

"Of course you would. So let's read Elder Maxwell's emphasis on dealing with the problem you had during your interviews back home."

Elder Curtis cleared his throat and read:

> There can be no repentance without recognition of wrong. Whether by provocation, introspection, or wrenching remembrance, denial must be dissolved. As with the prodigal son who finally "came to himself" (Luke 15:7), the first rays of *recognition* help us begin to see "things as they really are" (Jacob 4:13), including distinguishing between the motes and beams. Recognition is a sacred moment, often accompanied by the hot blush of shame.[5]

"Thank you, Elder. He pointed out that *recognition* is a sacred moment. And it is sacred, because it is at that turning point where we decide if we are going to accept the divine and kindly gift of godly sorrow and move forward and upward toward God or allow human pride and Satan to pull us down and away from God. Now if our discussion stopped here, one might assume that recognizing and admitting our sin and really feeling bad about it is the first step to repentance. And of course that is a big part of it, but there is something that must come even before that. Back home, there was something lacking even more important than the courage to confess. Can you tell me what it was?"

"No, I'm not sure that I can."

"Of course you can, Elder. Let's think about the fourth Article of Faith for a moment. It says that repentance is the *second* principle. But that principle won't work without being founded on the first principle, which is what?"

"Faith," he said.

"Good," praised the president, "but not quite complete."

The elder thought for a moment and then added, "Oh yeah, it's faith in the Lord Jesus Christ."

"That's right, but faith in *what* about Jesus Christ? It's not just faith that He exists or that He is the Son of God. It's a bigger and more important faith than that. What kind of faith in Christ do we need to have as a foundation for repentance, so that it actually results in a change of heart and forgiveness?"

The elder closed his eyes and pondered. Then he said, slowly, "I think it is faith that if I really repent, His Atonement will satisfy the demands of justice, and then His mercy can allow for my forgiveness without me having to pay the full price for whatever I did."

"Bingo!" exclaimed the president, patting him on the back. "It was only because you didn't have that faith yet that you could not find the courage to turn your burden over to the Lord. But that was then and now you are here, beginning the process. Without that faith in Christ, it is only natural to be more concerned about reputation than we are about being right with God. It is Satan's diabolical whispering that if we just stop doing our sin, without confession and full repentance, somehow it will all turn out okay. Now let's read this quote from President Benson."

Elder Curtis read:

> If we wish to truly repent and come unto Him so that we can be called members of His Church, we must first and foremost come to realize this eternal truth—the gospel plan is the plan of happiness. Wickedness never did, never does, never will bring us happiness. Violation of the laws of God brings only misery, bondage, and darkness. . . . If it were not for the perfect, sinless life of the Savior, which He willingly laid down for us, there could be no remission of sins.
>
> *Therefore, repentance means more than simply a reformation of behavior.* Many men and women in the world demonstrate great willpower and self-discipline in overcoming bad habits and the weaknesses of the flesh. Yet at the same time they give no thought to the Master, sometimes even openly rejecting Him. *Such changes of behavior, even if in a positive direction, do not constitute true repentance.*
>
> *Faith in the Lord Jesus Christ is the foundation upon which sincere and meaningful repentance must be built.* If we truly seek to put away sin, we must first look to Him who is the Author of our salvation.[6]

Elder Curtis slowly looked up and thoughtfully reflected, "So that means that even if I had confessed, but without faith in Christ, it still wouldn't have cleansed me or brought me closer to God?"

The president replied, "Oh you might have felt a little bit better toward God, but like he explained, you would have only been a reformed person, not a redeemed person. I'm so glad we are having this discussion; because it just may be that your lack of faith in Christ was a greater problem than the lust you were hiding!

"Elder, let's wrap up this session with another scripture. Would you please read 2 Nephi 2:8 from your Book of Mormon?"

The elder opened his book and read: " 'Wherefore, how great the importance to make these things known unto the inhabitants of the earth, that they may know that there is no flesh that can dwell in the presence of God, save it be through the merits, and mercy, and grace of the Holy Messiah' (2 Nephi 2:8)."

The president added, "You might also want to make a note there to cross-reference this verse to Alma 22:14, where it says that 'since man had fallen he could not merit anything of himself.' "

"President, I really blew it, didn't I?" Elder Curtis lamented.

"Elder Curtis, in spite of our best intentions, all of us 'blow it' sometimes. But you did the best you knew how at the time. I believe that if you had understood the majesty of the gift of repentance that Christ is offering, you would never have shortcut the process. What is important now is that you have recognized your error and have started on the path of making it right. The thing to do is to continue learning and then decide what you can do now. Remember, as long as your attention is focused on the past, Christ will not be able to help you repair your present. The next thing to do is to study this article, which compares godly sorrow and guilt, or worldly sorrow. Then . . ."

President Love was interrupted by a knock on the door. It was his wife. "Sorry, dear, but it is time for lunch. Will you be joining us?"

"What do you think, Elder? Are you ready for some physical nourishment?"

Elder Curtis answered with a big grin, and they enjoyed lunch with the family.

NOTES

1 Kimball, *The Miracle of Forgiveness*, 150.

2 Ibid., 157.

3 Ibid., 154.

4 Ibid., 155.

5 Neal A. Maxwell, "Repentance," *Ensign*, Nov. 1991, 30–31; emphasis in original.

6 Ezra Taft Benson, "A Mighty Change of Heart," *Ensign*, Oct. 1989, 2; emphasis added.

Godly Sorrow and Worldly Sorrow

After lunch, Elder Curtis went downstairs and back to the cubicle for more study. While Sister Richardson updated the president on some phone calls he needed to answer, the elder began to read his second assignment.

Godly Sorrow and Worldly Sorrow

Everyone who does wrong should have feelings of guilt and remorse. Such feelings are a gift of God, sent through our conscience. Feelings of guilt are the natural, divinely intended consequence of improper thoughts and actions. But all guilt is not the same. Some feelings of guilt are healthy and productive, motivating repentance and growth, while others, influenced by Satan, are unhealthy and spiritually destructive.

One day as I stepped outside onto our second-story deck to the backyard, I noticed that my neighbor was cleaning her yard of dog messes. Judging by her two large dogs' wildly wagging tails, it appeared that they were expecting some fun activity, but they were soon disappointed. With each pile she found, she shouted at them, "Bad dog!" For some reason, she grew increasingly angry at each pile she picked up. Each time she screamed "bad dog," their heads hung lower and their tails, which had only moments ago been wagging in anticipation, hung increasingly limp and motionless. The dogs' despair reminded me of the way Satan sidetracks our sincere efforts to repent with his discouraging whispers. It amazed me that my neighbor was condemning her dogs for doing what dogs have to do. I don't know what she expected them to do when nature called, but it was obvious that she was using shame and intimidation to manipulate their behavior. That is what Satan does. A loving Father does not use such negative tools to force you to do what is right. It is significant that Mormon used the same words, *invite* and *entice*, to describe the efforts of both the Lord and the devil to influence our feelings and priorities. "That which is of God inviteth and enticeth to do good continually," while "the devil is an enemy unto God, and fighteth against him continually, and inviteth and enticeth to sin, and to do that which is evil continually" (Moroni 7:13, 12).

The feelings of guilt that God sends through our conscience are both timed and proportioned to give us pause, to invite, to motivate, and to encourage us to repent and come closer to Him. The scriptures describe these divinely inspired feelings as "godly sorrow." They are both positive and healthy. But feelings of guilt can also be dangerous, because Satan and his demons are very skilled in hijacking what started out as godly sorrow and degrading it into something dark and destructive, like the "bad dog, shame-on-you!" pattern of my neighbor. While genuine remorse is always the beginning of sincere repentance, those kinds of shameful, demeaning feelings do not motivate repentance but only pull us downward into crippling despair and self-loathing.

Elder Curtis paused, realizing that that was exactly where he had been for the last six months. But now that he had gotten himself into that situation, how was he going to get out? Silently he prayed for better understanding and then continued reading.

Paul summarized these opposing feelings when he elaborated, "Now I rejoice, not that ye were made sorry, but that ye sorrowed to repentance: for ye were made sorry after a godly manner, that ye might receive damage by us in nothing. [Their discipleship was not harmed, but improved by his teachings and challenges.] For godly sorrow worketh [prompts or motivates] repentance to salvation not to be repented of [regretted]: but the sorrow of the world [discourages and] worketh death" (2 Corinthians 7:9–10).

The first recorded scriptural account of someone disobeying and then responding improperly to their feelings of guilt was Adam and Eve in the Garden of Eden. Following their partaking of the forbidden fruit, the Lord came into the garden and "called unto Adam, and said unto him, Where art thou?" Showing his inexperience with guilt, Adam said, "I heard thy voice in the garden, and I was afraid, because I was naked; and I hid myself" (Genesis 3:9–10). It is precisely this kind of worldly sorrow that Satan promotes, because it uses fear and shame to drive us away from the Lord instead of helping us to turn and repent.

One of two things will happen to every person who disobeys God. Either they will be drawn back to Him with humble and contrite remorse, intent on repentance and with hearts that are broken for being less obedient than they meant to be, or they will follow the "natural-man" trait of slinking away with unresolved guilt, looking for ways to hide from God.

Let's examine the godly sorrow that should follow recognition, or admission of sin, with President Spencer W. Kimball's words: "There must be more than a verbal acknowledgement. There must be an inner conviction giving to the sin its full diabolical weight. There must be increased devotion and much thought and study. There must be a re-awakening, a fortification, a re-birth" (*The Miracle of Forgiveness*, 155). In other words, recognizing and feeling bad about our sin is not enough. Sincere remorse for sin will motivate us to change. He also said, "Often people indicate that they have repented when all they have done is to express regret for a wrong act. But true repentance is marked by that godly sorrow that changes, transforms, and saves. To be sorry is not enough" (*The Miracle of Forgiveness*, 153).

Elder Curtis paused again, recognizing where he had fallen short by his efforts to cover his sin. He thought, *Now that I realize what I've done to myself, I've got to figure out how to undo it.* He realized that just running away from his mission was not going to fix anything. It was going to take a lot more than that. He resumed his reading.

President Kimball also warned of the danger of getting stuck in looking back and feeling guilty when he said, "Of course, even the conviction of guilt is not enough. It could be devastating and destructive were it not accompanied by efforts to rid oneself of guilt.

Accompanying the conviction, then, must be an earnest desire to clean up the guilt and compensate for the loss sustained through the error" (*The Miracle of Forgiveness*, 159). "Devastating and destructive" describe exactly the tools Satan uses to distort our sincere remorse and feelings of sorrow.

If we are not aware of Satan's efforts to hijack our feelings of godly sorrow, he may persuade us that clinging to guilt is a good substitute for proper repentance. We will then be held hostage by his diabolical distortion that the more guilty we feel, the more repentant and holy we are! What a terrible misrepresentation of a divine gift. As Elder Neal A. Maxwell emphasized, "He who was thrust down in the first estate delights to have us put ourselves down. Self-contempt is of Satan; there is none of it in heaven. We should, of course, learn from our mistakes, but without forever studying the instant replays as if these were the game of life itself" ("Notwithstanding My Weakness," *Ensign*, Nov. 1976, 14).

The problem for many of us is that it is easier to punish ourselves than it is to rely upon the Savior's mercy and forgiveness. Instead of surrendering our guilt to the Savior as we repent, we cling to it like a ball and chain, dragging our past and our guilt with us everywhere we go. Such preoccupation with past mistakes locks in guilt and locks out forgiveness. We think we are being crushed by the demands of justice when it is only our own failure to move past our guilt and to take advantage of the Atonement. Elder Richard G. Scott cautioned: "To continue to suffer when there has been proper repentance is not prompted by the Savior but the master of deceit, whose goal is to bind and enslave you. Satan will press you to continue to relive the details of past mistakes, knowing that such thoughts make forgiveness seem unattainable. In this way Satan attempts to tie strings to the mind and body so that he can manipulate you like a puppet" ("Peace of Conscience and Peace of Mind," *Ensign*, Nov. 2004, 18).

Though an essential part of repentance is to look back and regret what we did wrong, it is not part of repentance to punish ourselves with self-deprecating "bad dog" condemnations. If we liken sin to a gulf of unworthiness that separates us from God, then repentance is the bridge that will get us across the gulf. Too many times, however, when we discover our need for the bridge, we work at punishing ourselves for needing it instead of just crossing the bridge. Crossing that bridge should be a wonderful, joyful experience, a part of our ongoing journey in coming to Christ. The godly sorrow we should feel for our sins is like an intersection where we can correct the direction of our lives. It is not a place to set up camp and beat on ourselves.

A proper response to godly sorrow is much like saying "I'm sorry" to someone you have hurt. The more you love that someone, the quicker you are to say, "I'm sorry," and the quicker you are to make it right. Godly sorrow means that we recognize the harm our sinfulness does to our relationship with God. Thus, we eagerly seek to reconcile ourselves to Him through repentance.

Godly sorrow is not only what we feel *after* we have sinned. It is higher and nobler than that. It grows into an attitude of "I will give away all my sins to know thee" (Alma 22:18). It prompts a willing eagerness to lay everything on the altar of sacrifice. It is a yearning to be more like Christ and a sorrow that we are not, yet. It is also the regret and sorrow of knowing that because we are still human and fallen, we will probably sin again, in spite of our best efforts. It is a desire not only to avoid sin, but to not *want* to sin—a sorrow for mortal sinfulness. Finally, godly sorrow is a prayerful yearning, like Nephi's, to abhor sin and to "make me that I may shake at the appearance of sin" (2 Nephi 4:31).

Elder Curtis remembered that during all those torturous months when he had forced himself to avoid the pornography, he had felt no godly sorrow, only a longing to go back to the evil pleasures. Suddenly, he was ashamed in a new way—and it did not feel good.

Further Discussion on
Godly Sorrow and Guilt

After reading the article, Elder Curtis wandered through the office, wishing he did not have to continue confronting these issues. After a few minutes, he resigned himself to it and returned to the president's office. President Love looked up from the correspondence he was reading and invited him to sit down. He said, "So, Elder Curtis, what did you learn from what you just read?"

The elder replied, "I guess the part I liked the best was what Elder Maxwell taught about focusing on the instant replays, instead of letting the past go into the hands of the Savior and moving on with your life. I feel so ashamed for the way I handled things with my priesthood leaders."

The president replied kindly, "You already felt bad about that when you came in this morning. My purpose in having you study the article was not to make you feel worse but to arouse a different kind of remorse, the godly sorrow that will help you on the road back to the Savior."

The elder complained, "Okay, I'm confused. How can we know if our feelings of guilt are godly or worldly, healthy or harmful?"

The president replied, "Elder, the way to tell is incredibly simple.

True remorse, or the 'godly sorrow' that Paul talked about will always move us to repentance. It will invite us toward God with encouragement to make things right with Him and any others we may have harmed or offended. Whereas the counterfeit, worldly guilt—the distorted, over-emphasized 'bad dog' kind of self-condemning guilt—pulls us down. It makes us want to hide and cover things up. It builds barriers between us and God."

"I don't know if I'll ever get it right. Maybe it's too late for me now. My life's a mess."

The president replied, "Elder, you are doing fine. It is never too late for someone who sincerely wants to change and make things right. In another session we'll talk more about falling for Satan's whispered 'it's-too-late' and 'you'll-never-be-able-to change' lies. Don't feel bad if the whole picture is not clear to you right now. We've barely cracked the door open. We've got a lot more to learn, and we'll be doing it together. For now, I just want you to know that responding to godly sorrow with real repentance is a skill that improves with experience. It requires faith and hope that with our steady and consistent effort, the Savior will, step-by-step, lift us above our natural fallen selves into a new creature with a new nature and a new heart, molded in His image. It is not a one-time event, but a process. It is a realistic and patient, inching forward process, maybe stumbling along the way, but having a determination not to quit.

"We'll be talking more later about the process of making actual improvement in our characters. But for now," he continued, "I want you to understand what Alma meant when he taught his son to 'Let your sins trouble you, with that trouble which shall bring you down unto repentance' (Alma 42:29). This means that without going into the depths of despair we become quickly responsive to the godly sorrow we feel from our conscience. One of the keys that will help us to be more successful in this procedure is to lower our conscience threshold. Then when we are sensitive and in tune we can respond to the slightest nudge from the Holy Ghost. Life is a lot better when we don't need to be hit with a sledgehammer of guilt to prod us into changing. This is a skill we develop with practice."

The president sighed, knowing they must now enter a more complex doctrinal discussion. He explained, "Elder, the godly sorrow we have been talking about is not a specialized skill at feeling super guilty.

Rather, it is learning to feel sorrow for the proper things, and that may not be as obvious as it sounds. One reason that so many people get trapped in negative, self-defeating guilt patterns is because of misplaced blame. If we assume that every mistake we make and every sin we do is because we are wicked and loathsome in the sight of the Lord; it is easy to get sidetracked by the 'shame-on-me' kind of guilt. So the next thing we need to learn is to separate our real, spiritual identity from the fallen body that we inhabit. This is important because, in many cases, it is not *you* fighting *yourself*—it is you fighting your mortal, fallen nature, and oh, what a difference this can make. Elder Melvin J. Ballard emphasized how important it is to recognize the difference between our real, spirit identities and the bodies of fallen flesh that we wear."

He opened his resource drawer, pulled out a paper, and handed it to the elder. "Here," he said. "I want you to read Elder Ballard's words."

Elder Curtis read:

> The greatest conflict that any man or woman will ever have will be the battle that is had with self. I should like to speak of spirit and body as *"me"* and *"it."* "Me" is the individual who dwells in this body, who lived before I had such a body, and who will live when I step out of the body. *"It"* is the house I live in, the tabernacle of flesh and the great conflict is between *"me"* and *"it."*[1]

The President went on, "Here's another way to think about this principle of separation. If your car develops a mechanical defect, you don't condemn *yourself* for it because the car is not *you*; it is just something you ride in. So you get it repaired and get on with life. Unfortunately, however, we have become prone to identifying with the defects in our mortal tabernacles. By making us feel guilty for being human and imperfect, the devil diminishes our feelings of self-respect, self-worth, and confidence in our ability to rise above our fallen condition. This has been a very difficult lesson for me personally, but I think I have finally learned that it is not wise to blame myself or others for being a natural man. We inherited this condition by being born into this fallen world. The enemy is our fallen nature, not ourselves."

The elder protested, "That sounds a lot like 'the-devil-made-me-do-it' excuse some people use to excuse their sins."

The President replied patiently, "No, elder, it is not like that at all.

Actually, I'm glad you brought that up, because there is such an important difference, as I am about to explain. Alma tells us how this began when Adam and Eve transgressed and were driven from the Garden of Eden to begin their mortal probation." Opening his scriptures to Alma 42, he said, "Here, look at verse six with me. You see where it says that when Adam and Eve were sent out from the Garden of Eden 'they became fallen man.' All right, now verses nine and ten." He read portions of the two verses: " 'The fall had brought upon all mankind a spiritual death as well as a temporal, that is, they were cut off from the presence of the Lord. . . . [and] they had become carnal, sensual, and devilish, by nature, [so] this probationary state became a state for them to prepare; it became a preparatory state' (Alma 42:9–10)."

The President asked, "Did you notice that he did not say this is a time to hate or condemn ourselves for being human and having weaknesses or sins? He taught that mortality is a time to practice rising above our faults. Mortal probation is a time to learn and rise higher than our natural, fallen nature. Elder, would you agree that Heavenly Father is the supreme intelligence in the universe?"

"Of course."

"He is perfection, the ultimate of all that we can be, both physically and spiritually. Our physical bodies are precious and should be reverenced and respected, if for no other reason than they are created 'in the image of his own body' (Moses 6:9). But the bodies you and I dwell in *now* are not the same as the perfect bodies that He created. When Adam and Eve fell and were cast from the Garden of Eden, we, their posterity, inherited lesser bodies, bodies that are fallen and naturally predisposed to be carnal, sensual, devilish, and in a state that is contrary to eternal happiness. This means that *they* and every spirit to follow them into physical, mortal bodies becomes *subject to the carnal nature* that curses mortal flesh with the desires and tendencies of the natural man. I want you to learn more about this."

Reaching into his resource drawer, he found another folder and obtained an article entitled "The Problem We All Inherited." He handed it to the elder, saying, "Elder Curtis, here is your next homework assignment. Understanding these consequences of the Fall changes our entire perspective from one of struggling to overcome our evil selves to one of being rescued by the Savior. You need to gain the faith that through His Atonement, He can change us from the carnal, sensual, and devilish nature, in which we are now trapped, to one of holiness. Go back to your cubicle now, and get to work on this subject."

NOTES

1 "Struggle For The Soul," *New Era*, Mar. 1984, 35; emphasis added.

The Problem We All Inherited

*E*lder Curtis moved his chair by the window, where the afternoon sun gave more light. He sat and began to read.

The Problem We All Inherited

President Spencer W. Kimball observed, "Generally, *the evil way is the easier*, and since man is carnal, that way will triumph unless there be a conscious and a consistently vigorous effort to reject the evil and follow the good" (*The Miracle of Forgiveness*, 15). There is a constant war between *our* will—that is, the will of our divine spirit entities—and the will of our mortal bodies of flesh that have desires of their own, entirely independent of our own personal will and choice (see 2 Nephi 10:24). We live in a fallen world. As fallen beings, who are more likely to sin than not to sin, we have actually been described as enemies to God!

> For the natural man is an enemy to God, and has been from the fall of Adam, and will be, forever and ever, unless he yields to the enticings of the Holy Spirit, and putteth off the natural man and becometh a saint through the atonement of Christ the Lord, and becometh as a child, submissive, meek, humble, patient, full of love, willing to submit to all things which the Lord seeth fit to inflict upon him, even as a child doth submit to his father. (Mosiah 3:19)

"And thus we see," said Alma, "that *all mankind* were fallen, and they were in the grasp of justice; yea, the justice of God, which consigned them forever to be cut off from his presence" (Alma 42:10; emphasis added). He further emphasized that every mortal being (including prophets and apostles), needs to be rescued from this fallen condition. "For it is expedient that an atonement should be made; for according to the great plan of the Eternal God there must be an atonement made, or else *all mankind* must unavoidably perish; yea, all are hardened; yea, all are fallen and are lost, and must perish except it be through the atonement which it is expedient should be made" (Alma 34:9; emphasis added).

The brother of Jared emphasized the same plight. He prayed, "Now behold, O Lord, and do not be angry with thy servant because of his weakness before thee; for we know that thou art holy and dwellest in the heavens, and that we are unworthy before thee; *because of the fall our natures have become evil continually*; nevertheless, O Lord, thou hast given us a commandment that we must call upon thee, that from thee we may receive according to our desires" (Ether 3:2; emphasis added). The devil often tricks a repentant person into feeling false and distorted guilt by persuading them that their sin makes them unique, as if they were the only person, or the worst person ever to do that sin. But sin is not unique to any person, "For all have sinned, and come short of the glory of God" (Romans 3:23).

Elder Curtis though that in spite of what the article claimed, he was pretty sure there weren't very many elders, if any, who had come on a mission with such a dark secret as his. He continued reading.

Every person who ever came to this earth has to struggle against the desires of a fallen nature. We are all spirit children of God who are in a mortal school, learning how to overcome the fallen flesh so that we may prepare to return to His presence. As President Joseph Fielding Smith taught:

> There isn't one of us . . . that hasn't done something wrong and then been sorry and wished we hadn't. Then our consciences strike us and we have been very, very miserable. Have you gone through that experience? I have. But here we have the Son of God carrying the burden of my transgressions and your transgressions and the transgressions of every soul that receives the gospel of Jesus Christ. I added something to it; so did you. So did everybody else. (*The Life & Teachings of Jesus and His Apostles*, 175–76).

Even the great King Benjamin said, "I am like as yourselves, subject to all manner of infirmities in body and mind" (Mosiah 2:11). And the mighty Nephi, who was such an example of righteousness and steadfast dependability, lamented: "O wretched man that I am! Yea, my heart sorroweth because of my flesh; my soul grieveth because of mine iniquities. I am encompassed about, because of the temptations and the sins which do so easily beset me" (2 Nephi 4:17–18).

Both Peter and Paul spoke of this battle between our spirits and our fallen nature: "Dearly beloved, I beseech you as strangers and pilgrims, abstain from fleshly lusts, *which war against the soul*" (1 Peter 2:11; emphasis added). Paul explained: "For the flesh lusteth against the Spirit, and the Spirit against the flesh: and these are contrary the one to the other: *so that ye cannot do the things that ye would*" (Galatians 5:17; emphasis added). Because of this dilemma, and no matter how sincerely we try to avoid sin, "There is never a day in any man's life when repentance is not essential to his well-being and eternal progress" (Spencer W. Kimball, *The Miracle of Forgiveness*, 32).

We may not like it, but to grow spiritually and rise above our fallen nature, we must recognize that for now and throughout our mortal probation our fallen nature and our mortal flesh have desires and traits that we don't like and wish we didn't have. Recognizing this reality is part of the godly sorrow that motivates us to reach beyond our present limitations. Our faith is in Christ, who has promised that we can all learn to overcome our imperfections and rise above them with His help. We must turn to Christ for rescue because no one can lift himself from a fallen nature by determination, willpower, or good works alone. As Aaron taught the Lamanites: "And since man had fallen he could not merit anything of himself; but the sufferings and death of Christ atone for their sins, through faith and repentance" (Alma 22:14).

Once again, Elder Curtis hesitated before returning to the president's office. He wondered, *Just how is this concept supposed to help me? I already knew that I'm fallen. I'm very fallen. That's my problem—I'm so fallen that I love sin.*

Further Discussion on
Being Fallen

Elder Curtis returned to the president's office and complained, "Wow, now I'm really confused. All day you've been teaching me about guilt, and now you tell me to back off and make excuses for my sins. Which is it?"

The president was surprised and asked him how he reached that conclusion.

Elder Curtis explained, "First you emphasize all this godly sorrow stuff and that the guilty feelings that brought me in here to talk to you weren't good enough, even though they are driving me crazy. Now you say that because we are all fallen, we should expect to sin. I can't believe that my mission president is making excuses for sin!"

"Well now," replied the president, "I can see we need some clarification here. Sit down, Elder Curtis, and let's talk this through. To begin with, I'm glad to see that you are taking your study seriously and not just passively buying into everything I say without your own understanding and conviction. That's what we ask our investigators to do, and I'm glad you are doing the same.

"Now then, nothing that I said or wrote was excusing sin. The Lord declared that He cannot look upon any sin with the 'least degree' of allowance, and neither should we (see D&C 1:31). As Alma admonished, 'Do not endeavor to excuse yourself in the least point because of your sins, by denying the justice of God; but do you let the justice of God, and his mercy, and his long-suffering have full sway in your heart; and let it bring you down to the dust in humility' (Alma 42:30). There is the honest acknowledgement of the sinful nature that we all battle, along with our need for godly sorrow and the recognition of how much we need Christ to overcome ourselves. Alma also warned that we should not deliberately 'risk one more offense against your God' (Alma 41:9)."

He continued, "On the other hand, and perhaps even to our surprise, Nephi elaborated, 'Not that I would excuse myself because of other men, but because of the weakness which is in me, according to the flesh, I would excuse myself' (1 Nephi 19:6). He wasn't excusing his sin, nor should we. But he recognized that, because of the fall, there are times when even our best intentions won't keep us perfectly on the straight and narrow path. There has to be a place for some patience, mercy, and compassion for our mortal inadequacies.

"It is true that when our conscience protests a certain thought or action, we need to feel deep and sincere remorse, or godly sorrow, for disobeying Heavenly Father and breaking our covenants. But we also need to have some compassion and mercy for ourselves because every bad thing that we do is not automatically done because we are wicked. In many cases it is because we are fallen and imperfect, and it is not helpful to label ourselves with condemnation and shame. We live in a telestial world. We live in bodies that are, by nature, carnal, sensual, and devilish and that want to make us do things that are contrary to the Spirit. That's why Elder Ballard explained that when we find ourselves wanting to sin and make lesser choices—even though we know better—it is helpful to recognize that the conflict is not *me* against *myself*, but *me* against *it*—the mortal body of flesh that I live in.

"I find it helpful to compare myself to an astronaut on a distant planet. I would have to wear a spacesuit to survive in that foreign environment, just as our spirits are here, wearing physical bodies. Would you agree with me that an astronaut would never confuse his *spacesuit* with his *personal identity*? And wouldn't you also agree that he would be aware at all times that the spacesuit he wears is merely a covering for the real person inside?"

The elder agreed.

"Well, it's the same with our physical bodies. Elder Ballard was not teaching us to make excuses for our sins but of the need to think of our physical bodies as something separate from ourselves, like a spacesuit worn by our spirit in this foreign environment of mortality. Now one of the spacesuit's jobs is to provide oxygen to the astronaut and then get rid of the carbon dioxide as he breathes. That was the design. If you were an astronaut on a mission to a faraway planet and your spacesuit—on its own and independent of your choice—began occasionally issuing carbon dioxide instead of oxygen, that would be backwards to the design. But would you let that malfunction make you go into spasms of self-condemnation, wondering why you were such an awful person for living inside a spacesuit that was not perfect? Of course not. You would recognize that nothing in our mortal world is perfect. You would simply take the defective spacesuit to the repair technician."

The president continued, "You and I fought a premortal war for the privilege of coming here to dwell in physical bodies during this earthly school. The problem is that we all have defective spacesuits, fallen bodies that are constantly trying to pull us away from things that promote spiritual growth. We never make excuses for sin. But instead of condemning ourselves for being fallen, or defective, our job is to take ourselves to the Divine Repairman—the Savior—the only One who can fix the flaws in our mortal natures. Aren't we thankful that He has invited us to bring all of our defects to Him for repair? This is one of the keys to healing and to being born again."

He asked the elder, "Does this make more sense to you now?"

Elder Curtis still had reservations, but he replied slowly, "I think so, but I need more time to think about it. I'm just not used to all these nuances about guilt."

The president replied, "Elder, perhaps you are not used to the idea of how easily Christ could take your guilt from you, if you would only surrender your feelings and yourself to Him who can heal all things." He continued, "Let me put this in very personal terms. Knowing that I sin because I live in a fallen body doesn't lessen my sorrow for my sin, but it changes the blame that I am sorry for. Of course I am sorry for the sin itself, because I never want to do anything to break my covenants or to disappoint the Lord. But beyond that, I am even sorrier that I am still subject to my fallen nature.

"Yes, I want to overcome every bad habit or sinful desire, but even more than that, I want to overcome my sinful nature. I not only want to stop doing any specific sin, but I also want to stop desiring sin in the first place. I want to be more faithful in keeping my covenants. I want Heavenly Father to be able to trust me. I want to be able to trust myself. I want to abhor sin rather than having to struggle to resist it all the time. In other words, my daily, continual repentance is bigger than any specific sin. It reaches higher, striving to become Christlike and receive the mighty change of heart that only He can put within me as I become increasingly obedient and trusting of His grace and power."

The president paused and then said, "You know, one of my favorite pastimes is watching construction sites. I find it fascinating to watch how everything comes together over time to create whatever edifice it is that they are building. I mention that because I've noticed that every construction site has one thing in common. There is always one or more of those Port-O-Potty kind of outhouses at the site. Have you noticed that too?"

"Of course, but I don't see what that has to do with godly sorrow or being fallen."

"But, Elder, it has everything to do with it. First of all, the workers do not feel shame for needing a toilet. It is just part of being human, just like making mistakes and learning the better way. And second, the construction company, while not rejoicing in the waste products of their workers, have made arrangements for it because until they can find perfect, resurrected workers, there has to be a provision made for their humanness."

"Okay, okay, I can see your point. But what does that have to do with our discussion?"

"What it has to do with it is that God knew that the moment His children fell into mortality there were going to be sins. And so there had to be a provision made to rescue His children from those sins and from the consequences of those sins. Repentance and forgiveness weren't added to the plan as an afterthought. They were part of the plan from the very beginning." He looked through a stack of *Ensigns*, selected one, browsed for a moment, and then requested, "Listen to what Elder Richard G. Scott taught about this. 'Knowing that all of

His spirit children save His Only Begotten, Jesus Christ, would unintentionally or intentionally violate His laws, our Eternal Father provided a means to correct the consequences of such acts. Whether the violation be great or small, the solution is the same: full repentance through faith in Jesus Christ and His Atonement with obedience to His commandments.'[1]

"You should know, Elder Curtis, that the first recorded revelation that God sent to Adam was about the plan of repentance (see Moses 4:6–8). So we should not be ashamed for needing to repent of something any more than we should be ashamed of our bodily need to discard its waste material." With that, he pulled another article from his resource drawer and sent the elder out to study again.

NOTES

1 "Peace of Conscience and Peace of Mind," *Ensign*, Nov. 2004, 16.

Blessed Are the Repentant

*T*he cubicle was noisy because of some missionaries discussing car repairs with Elder Richardson, so Elder Curtis got his scriptures and went upstairs to the living room. He felt grateful for the quiet he found there and began to read.

Blessed Are the Repentant

When Satan sees that we are determined to repent, he frequently makes us feel ashamed for needing repentance. (Always, always, he is trying to put barriers between God's love and us.) But rather than something shameful, repentance is proof that we are progressing, learning a better way, and moving in the direction Father wants us to go. That is why we came to this earth school. As Jeffrey R. Holland observed, "Repentance is not a foreboding word. It is, following faith, the most encouraging word in the Christian vocabulary. Repentance is simply the scriptural invitation for growth and improvement and progress and renewal" ("For Times of Trouble," *New Era*, Oct. 1980, 11).

Because learning from our mistakes is such an important part of this mortal experience, repentance was planned and prepared as a key ingredient of earth life. Alma pointed out, "The way is prepared that whosoever will may walk therein and be saved" (Alma 41:8). And Nephi indicated, "The Lord knoweth all things from the beginning [including the fact that we would all sin]; wherefore, he prepareth a way to accomplish all his works among the children of men" (1 Nephi 9:6). The way that God prepared did not depend upon us walking in perfect obedience, even though we all strive toward that goal, but upon *walking in repentance* as a means of turning away from poor choices and toward the Lord through better choices and actions. As BYU professor Robert L. Millet stated, "The climb of spirituality is seldom a straight and steady movement up the mountain; it is, more likely than not, punctuated with detours and side canyons, wasted time and effort, slips and stumbles. That's because most of us grow gradually, not exponentially" (*Are We There Yet?*, 112–113).

Many scriptures characterize the gospel of Jesus Christ as "the gospel of repentance." For example, when Joseph Smith and Oliver Cowdery received the Aaronic Priesthood, Oliver reported, "On a sudden, as from the midst of eternity, the voice of the Redeemer spake peace to us, while the veil was parted and the angel of God came down clothed with glory, and delivered the anxiously looked for message, and *the keys of the Gospel of repentance*" (JS—H footnote; emphasis added). Part of the actual, official words used by John the Baptist in conferring that priesthood were, "Upon you my fellow servants, in the name of Messiah I confer the Priesthood of Aaron, which holds the keys of the ministering of angels, and of the gospel of repentance" (D&C 13:1). In a First Presidency message on repentance, Spencer W. Kimball emphasized this same characterization.

> We are so grateful that our Heavenly Father has blessed us with *the gospel of repentance.* It is central to all that makes up the gospel plan. Repentance is the Lord's law of growth, his principle of development, and his plan for happiness. . . .
>
> Thus, the mission of The Church of Jesus Christ of Latter-day Saints is to call people everywhere to repentance so that they might know the joys of gospel living. How grateful we are that our Heavenly Father has given us the gift of repentance. ("The Gospel of Repentance," *Ensign*, Oct. 1982, 2; emphasis added)

Rather than shaming us for needing repentance, the Lord emphasized that this is His gospel plan. And as we follow that plan, He assures, "Blessed are they who will repent and hearken unto the voice of the Lord their God; *for these are they that shall be saved*" (Helaman 12:23; also 13:11, 13; emphasis added). He also revealed, "Blessed is he whose transgression is forgiven, whose sin is covered"

(Romans 4:7; also Psalm 32:1). Nowhere do the scriptures say, or even hint, "Blessed is he who never needs to repent or receive forgiveness." Only Christ was in that position. The Lord's plan does not demand flawless performance but makes provision for our learning to choose between good and evil as we learn the better way, grow and improve, correct our mistakes, and solidify our resolve to become more obedient. Thus, President Spencer W. Kimball concluded that "repentance is for every soul who has not yet reached perfection" and that "repentance and forgiveness are part of the glorious climb toward godhood" (*The Miracle of Forgiveness*, 33, 14).

As we struggle to keep our covenants more faithfully, we are encouraged to know that those disciples who need repentance are not the exception in God's family but the expected 100 percent majority. "Wherefore teach it unto your children, that *all men*, everywhere, must repent, or they can in nowise inherit the kingdom of God, for no unclean thing can dwell there, or dwell in his presence" (Moses 6:57; emphasis added). And we rejoice in the Lord's promise that "as often as my people repent will I forgive them their trespasses against me" (Mosiah 26:30; see also Alma 5:33, Moroni 6:8). It is Satan's falsification that the only ones who will make it into the celestial kingdom will be those who need little or no repentance! The Savior taught that the purpose of the gospel and the Church is for "the convincing of many of their sins, that they may come unto repentance, *and that they may come unto the kingdom of my Father*" (D&C 18:44; emphasis added).

Nature provides many spiritual symbols. For example, these trees show evidence of having made some rather dumb choices in their growth. Just like people who mess up their lives, these trees got off the "strait and narrow path" upward, toward the sky and light. Rather than a symbol of perverted trees, however, they reflect the hope that if even a tree can repent and get back on the right path, so can we.

Just as we are not angry about the mistakes the trees made, but are glad that they finally got it right, our moving closer to the Lord through repentance does not bring sadness to Him, but joy and rejoicing. "Behold, I say unto you that your brethren in Zion begin to repent, and the angels rejoice over them" (D&C 90:34).

> What man of you, having an hundred sheep, if he lose one of them, doth not leave the ninety and nine in the wilderness, and go after that which is lost, until he find it?
>
> And when he hath found it, he layeth it on his shoulders, rejoicing.
>
> And when he cometh home, he calleth together his friends and neighbours, saying unto them, Rejoice with me; for I have found my sheep which was lost.
>
> I say unto you, that likewise joy shall be in heaven over one sinner that repenteth, more than over ninety and nine just persons, which need no repentance. (Luke 15:4–7)

Elder Curtis put down the paper and pondered. *I am so confused,* he thought. *This article almost sounds like repentance is something to be proud of. But that can't be right.* He decided to read through it again before going back to the president.

Further Discussion on
the Gospel of Repentance

$\mathscr{E}$lder Curtis was still unsure, even after the second reading. Once again he returned to the president's office. He said, "President, first you told me that I didn't repent properly before my mission. I admit that. But all my life I've heard talks about how we should not casually justify sinning because it seems so easy to repent. They say how much better it is not to sin in the first place, rather than to deliberately do something bad and then figure you can just quickly fix it up with repentance."

"Good for you, Elder Curtis. That is absolutely true. Do you have your copy of the *For the Strength of Youth* pamphlet with you?"

"Yes," said the Elder, pulling it from his scripture bag.

"Then let's have you read from the section on repentance." After the president pointed out the paragraph he wanted, the elder read:

> Some people knowingly break God's commandments, expecting to repent before they go to the temple or serve a mission. Such deliberate sin mocks the Savior's Atonement and invites Satan to influence your life. Repentance for such behavior is difficult and can take a long time. If you sin in this way, you may lose years of blessings and spiritual guidance. You may become trapped in the sinful behavior,

making it difficult to find your way back.[1]

"Yes," said the elder, "that's exactly what I'm talking about."

"Good, then we are in agreement. Unfortunately, there does seem to be a growing trend of thinking you can have your fun by disobeying the commandments—especially the Word of Wisdom and the laws of chastity—and then expect to just patch it up, as you described. And there have been lots of talks about that recently. Repentance is neither easy nor quick, and people would not think that way if they remembered the warning that God will not be mocked (see Galatians 6:7; D&C 63:58). So what is the problem?"

Frustrated, the elder protested, "Well, your article almost makes it seem like we should be proud that we sinned so that we can then follow the plan of repentance. But that can't be right. If it is okay with God that we all need repentance over and over for our whole lives, why did He even put us here on probation, anyway? Why not just 'swish,' and make us all good and put us into the celestial kingdom to live happily ever after?"

The president sighed, but he smiled as he replied, "Elder, surely you know the answer to that question. Even though God is all-powerful, there is one thing that is impossible to Him, and that is to violate our agency. Of course He wants us all to be with Him in the celestial kingdom, but if He were to put us there before we are qualified, we would be more miserable than we would be in hell!

"There were people in Moroni's time with the same question. To them he challenged, 'Do ye suppose that ye shall dwell with him under a consciousness of your guilt? Do ye suppose that ye could be happy to dwell with that holy Being, when your souls are racked with a consciousness of guilt that ye have ever abused his laws? Behold, I say unto you that ye would be more miserable to dwell with a holy and just God, under a consciousness of your filthiness before him, than ye would to dwell with the damned souls in hell' (Mormon 9:3–4).

"God doesn't want us to sin and then have to repent, but that is the reality of living in a fallen world as a natural man, so He made it a part of the plan from the beginning. The reason repentance is so crucial to the gospel plan is so that we have a way to slowly, incrementally grow and improve and have our natures changed so that someday, it will be perfectly natural and appropriate for us to be in His presence, because we will have become like Him (see 1 John 3:2; Moroni 7:48). But that will never happen as long as a person disrespects the Lord and the gospel by deliberately flaunting their sinful ways in mockery of what this life is all about." Pulling a book from the nearby shelf, he opened it to a particular page and handed it to the elder. "Here," he said, "please read the marked passage. It is a simple summary from President Kimball."

The elder read, " 'Were it not for the blessed gifts of repentance and forgiveness this would be a hopeless situation for man, since no one except the Master has ever lived sinless on the earth.' "[2]

He gave the book back to the president who returned it to the shelf, saying, "There is something else here that we need to discuss. It seems to me that whenever someone mentions Isaiah's prophecy about 'a marvelous work and a wonder' in the last days, we often assume that it is referring to things like the Restoration of the Church, the fulness of the gospel, and the Book of Mormon" (see Isaiah 29:14).

"Well, doesn't it?" asked the elder, surprised at the turn in the conversation.

"Of course it does, but it is also talking about the wonder of repentance that helps us to rise above the fallen nature. Please turn to 2 Nephi 25 and read verse seventeen."

" 'And the Lord will set his hand again the second time to restore his people from their lost and fallen state. Wherefore, he will proceed to do a marvelous work and a wonder among the children of men' (2 Nephi 25:17)."

The confused elder asked, "So? That sounds exactly like the Restoration stuff we always hear about."

"Well, almost, except that this verse also emphasizes that the purpose of the marvelous work and a wonder is not just to restore the Church structure and authority, but also to recover His people from being lost and fallen. That is the purpose of the Church and the priesthood. But besides all that, exactly what *will* be the marvelous work and a wonder that will recover and lift His people above their fallen state? He gave us the answer in the Doctrine and Covenants."

Elder Curtis turned to section eighteen and read verse forty-four as instructed. " 'I will work a marvelous work among the children of men, unto the convincing of many of their sins, that they may come unto repentance, and that they may come unto the kingdom of my

Father' (D&C 18:44)." He began to see all of this in a new light.

"Elder," the president summarized, "it is easy to think of the dramatic repentance of people like Zeezrom or Alma and the sons of Mosiah as a marvelous work and a wonder. But the purpose of the Church, the gospel, and everything that we do is to help each person, one at a time, become convinced of their sins, move through the process of repentance, and ultimately, receive the 'born again' and 'mighty change' of heart experiences that molds them into the image and likeness of the Savior. Repentance and obedience are the way we come to Christ and receive forgiveness and cleansing.

"Elder Curtis, I can see why your mind is still not settled on this matter and I apologize. It is my fault, not yours." Reaching into his resource drawer again, he pulled another article and handed it to the elder. "I should have given you this second article at the same time as the last because it describes the second half of the plan of the gospel of repentance.

"Here's the thing—repentance alone will never erase sin and guilt. To finish that process we are all dependent upon the Savior, for He alone has the power to remove guilt. No matter how sincerely and totally we repent, only Jesus Christ has the authority to alter our status before the bar of justice. Repentance alone cannot do that.

"I wonder if you have heard about the son of a general authority who went to the mission field with his father. The son betrayed his calling and his fellow missionaries when he gave in to temptation and committed fornication. When this unthinkable sin became known and widely publicized, the reputation of the missionaries and the Church was destroyed. They had to pull all of the missionaries out of that area and close the mission."

The elder exclaimed, "Wow! How embarrassing! That's even worse than what I did. I am surprised that you would even talk about it."

"Not only can I talk about it, I can even name the people involved, because the father made it a part of the public Church record so that we could learn from it."

"I just can't believe that. I thought such things were totally confidential."

"Of course they are." President Love smiled and went on. "There is an interesting scripture in D&C 52:14 in which the Lord explained that one purpose of scripture is to give us 'a pattern in all things, that ye may not be deceived.' As you prepared for your mission, you were deceived into a incomplete, imitation repentance. The general authority whose son did this not only wanted to help his son to repent but also to give the rest of us a pattern for our own repentance and hope of forgiveness. Since he was the President of the Church at that time, I think he had the right to make that decision. The prophet's name was Alma, and his missionary son who was in such deep trouble was Corianton. Just because it happened more than two thousand years ago doesn't make it any less serious nor any less valuable as a pattern for our own repentance.

"Elder Curtis, I want you to go study this article now and see, when you put the Savior's powerful Atonement hand in hand with your part in the gospel's plan of repentance, if it doesn't make more sense to you."

NOTES

1 *For the Strength of Youth*, 30.

2 *The Miracle of Forgiveness*, 20.

He "Taketh Away"

The office was still noisy, so Elder Curtis decided to return to the living room upstairs. However, Sister Richardson told him that she needed his help first. She showed him some reports that Elder Brown had prepared for Salt Lake and asked him to make copies and mail them before he continued his studies. When he was done, he went back upstairs, anxious to read the next article.

He "Taketh Away"

As Isaiah looked forward to the coming ministry of the Savior, he described some of the blessings we could receive as we allowed Him to rescue us from our fallen nature. Speaking prophetically, as if he were Christ, he said, "the Lord [meaning Heavenly Father] hath anointed me to preach *good tidings* unto the meek" (Isaiah 61:1; emphasis added). An angel echoed this prophecy, as he announced the birth of Christ to the astonished shepherds, saying, "I bring you *good tidings of great joy*, which shall be to *all* people" (Luke 2:10; emphasis added). "All people" includes every person who is willing to repent and come to Christ.

This wording is so symbolic of the meaning of Christ's ministry that it was repeated by an angel to King Benjamin: "Behold, I am come to declare unto *you the glad tidings of great joy*" (Mosiah 3:3; emphasis added). And as Joseph and Sidney witnessed the vision that resulted in section seventy-six of the Doctrine and Covenants, they, too, heard an angel testify of those same "glad tidings." He explained that the good news was that Christ's mission was to bear our sins, to cleanse and sanctify us as we repent. The angel announced: "And this is the gospel, the glad tidings, which the voice out of the heavens bore record unto us—That he came into the world, even Jesus, to be crucified for the world, and to bear the sins of the world, and to sanctify the world, and to cleanse it from all unrighteousness" (D&C 76:40–41).

In beautiful simplicity, John echoed these prophecies when he proclaimed, "Behold the Lamb of God, which *taketh away* the sin of the world" (John 1:29; emphasis added). When the Lord spoke to Alma about the administration of the Church, He explained, "For behold, this is my church; whosoever is baptized shall be baptized unto repentance. And whomsoever ye receive shall believe in my name; and him will I freely forgive. *For it is I that taketh upon me the sins of the world*; for it is I that hath created them; and it is I that granteth unto him that believeth unto the end a place at my right hand" (Mosiah 26:23; emphasis added). And one of the first things that Christ stated to the Nephites when He appeared to them after His resurrection was this power and His goal to "take away" our sins: "And behold, I am the light and the life of the world; and I have drunk out of that bitter cup which the Father hath given me, and have glorified the Father *in taking upon me the sins of the world*" (3 Nephi 11:11; emphasis added).

"Take away." What a wonderful phrase. A converted Lamanite king used it to describe the miracle by which he and his people were cleansed of their guilt, shame, and remorse. "And I also thank my God, yea, my great God, that he hath granted unto us that we might repent of these things, and also that he hath forgiven us of those our many sins and murders which we have committed, and *taken away the guilt from our hearts*, through the merits of his Son" (Alma 24:10; emphasis added). To have the guilt removed from our hearts is surely the goal of every repentant person. After Enos had repented of his sins, "there came a voice unto [him], saying: Enos, thy sins are forgiven thee, and thou shalt be blessed." Enos "knew that God could not lie; wherefore, [his] guilt was swept away. And [he] said: Lord, how is it done?" The answer was: "Because of thy faith in Christ" (Enos 1:5–8).

It is abundantly clear that the "glad tidings" refer to Christ's power to "take away" our sins, to make us clean, and to guide us back to celestial glory with Him. It is also clear that it is upon these glad tidings that we base our hope and confidence that our sincere repentance will lead to redemption. These were the glad tidings that Corianton did not understand but that he learned from Alma.

As many times as he'd heard the Christmas story, Elder Curtis had never even thought about the angel's announcement of "good tidings of great joy." He'd only thought of that appearance as announcing Christ's birth—not actually the purpose of His mission. And he'd certainly never noticed how many times that phrase had been repeated throughout the scriptures. Truly it would be good tidings and a joyful thing if he could overcome his shame and feel right before the Lord. He folded his arms and prayed for that. Then he continued reading, hoping to understand and then apply the "pattern" that President Love had mentioned from Corianton's sin and repentance.

Corianton's sin presents one of the saddest stories in the Book of Mormon, as well as some of the best news of the book. It was Corianton's fornication with a harlot that prompted Alma's famous declaration that such sins of immorality are ranked second only to murder (see Alma 39:5; also Bruce C. Hafen, "The Gospel and Romantic Love," *New Era*, Feb. 2002, 10). Alma spared no words in teaching his son how abominable this sin was in the sight of God, and the serious jeopardy into which this had placed his soul. We can scarcely imagine his humiliation and shame. But Alma's purpose was not to leave his son in this embarrassing guilt and humiliation, but to teach him the way back as a pattern for us all. And so he connected his son's sins to the "glad tidings" that Christ can take away such horrible guilt and stain when we repent and come to Him in obedience.

Turning from a lengthy chastisement, the loving father began to give hope to his son. He stated, "And now, my son, I would say somewhat unto you concerning the coming of Christ. Behold, I say unto you, that it is he that surely shall come *to take away the sins of the world*; yea, he cometh to declare glad tidings of salvation unto his people" (Alma 39:15; emphasis added). Not only was that message meant to give hope to his son (who would, indeed, repent of his sins so completely that he would later become a Church leader described as a man of God—see Alma 48:18), but it was also the very message that Alma had originally wanted him to share with the Zoramites. He continued, "And now, my son, this was the ministry unto which ye were called, *to declare these glad tidings* unto this people, to prepare their minds; or rather that salvation might come unto them, that they may prepare the minds of their children to hear the word at the time of his coming" (Alma 39:16; emphasis added). This is the same ministry that has been given to missionaries in the restored Church. "Lift up your heart and rejoice, for the hour of your mission is come; and your tongue shall be loosed, and *you shall declare glad tidings of great joy* unto this generation" (D&C 31:3).

What incredible good news are the glad tidings that Christ can take away the sins and the guilt of every sincerely repentant person. Elder M. Russell Ballard described the danger of doubting these glad tidings when he warned:

> It is a lie propounded by the adversary that our sins can run too deep, that any one of us has sunk below the reach of the Savior and his atonement. The scriptures give us only one exception: those who have sinned against the Holy Ghost, "having crucified [the Savior] unto themselves and put him to an open shame" after having known the Lord's power and partaken of it (see D&C 76:31–37). If we do not fall into this category (and those who do are few), we *can*, with the help of the Lord, come back onto the path and become clean and pure again, worthy to receive our Father's greatest blessings. ("A Chance to Start Over: Church Disciplinary Councils and the Restoration of Blessings," *Ensign,* Sept. 1990, 19; emphasis in original)

And yet many sincere people are hesitant to ask for the Lord's forgiveness, even after full, sincere, and complete repentance. They may feel, perhaps subconsciously, that God is reluctant to forgive. But the truth is that He is always ready, even eager, to forgive. He is "a God ready to pardon, gracious and merciful, slow to anger, and of great kindness" (Nehemiah 9:17). The Lord addressed this prevalent attitude of regarding our God as vindictive, or as seeking opportunities to punish rather than forgive, when He asked, "Have I any pleasure at all that the wicked should die? Saith the Lord God: and not that he should return from his ways, and live?" (Ezekiel 18:23). Let us not forget that He is, after all, our Father, and He is always on our side. If we were to compare mortal life to a sporting event, we would not think of Heavenly Father and our Savior as the referees, who are always judging the details of each and every play and ever watching for the slightest infraction of the rules, but rather, as coaches, encouraging us to try again, assuring us that we can do better the next time.

Jesus Christ promised: "He that repents and does the commandments of the Lord *shall be forgiven*" (D&C 1:32; emphasis added). This is an ironclad, unconditional promise from the Son of God. As Elder Marion G. Romney emphasized, "Forgiveness is as wide as repentance. Every person will be forgiven for all the transgressions of which he truly repents. If he repents of all his sins, *he shall stand spotless before God* because of the atonement of our Master and Savior, Jesus Christ" (in Conference Report, Oct. 1955, 124; emphasis added).

The idea that he might actually, someday, stand *spotless* before the Lord almost took the elder's breath away. As he thought about such a possibility, he realized he had no idea of how to make that happen. But he was determined to find out. He continued reading, hoping for some practical clues that could begin to apply so that Christ could also "take away" his personal sin and guilt.

The difficulty in feeling forgiven after we repent is never because God is unwilling to forgive. His forgiveness is automatic. When we confess, repent, and obey, He forgives. If we cannot feel the Lord's forgiveness once we have repented and put our lives back in harmony with His commandments, it is because of our lack of faith in the glad tidings or the overwhelming presence of our own self-condemnation. When the Lord declared, "I, the Lord, will forgive whom I will forgive, but of you it is required to forgive all men," (D&C 64:10), He was referring to our obligation to forgive ourselves, as well as others. Referring to this scripture, Elder Theodore M. Burton elaborated, "I find here an answer for some who refuse to forgive themselves and who make themselves miserable by continually talking about their sins. They say, 'I just can't forgive myself for the things I have done.' I reply, 'Do you think you are more holy than the Lord? If He is willing to forgive you, shouldn't you be willing to forgive yourself now that you have repented of your sin?' " ("A Marriage to Last through Eternity," *Ensign*, Jun. 1987, 15).

Elder Richard G. Scott also commented on those who cannot forgive themselves for past transgressions, even when they know the Lord has forgiven them. He stressed that "suffering does not bring forgiveness. It comes through faith in Christ and obedience to his teachings, so that his gift of redemption can apply." He continued:

"Can't you see that to continue to suffer for sins, when there has been proper repentance and forgiveness of the Lord, is not prompted by the Savior but by the master of deceit, whose goal has always been to bind and enslave the children of our Father in Heaven? Satan would encourage you to continue to relive the details of past mistakes, knowing that such thoughts make progress, growth, and service difficult to attain" ("We Love You—Please Come Back," *Ensign*, May 1986, 10–11).

The scriptures use powerful symbolism to teach us how perfectly and completely Christ can "take away" or remove our sin following repentance. Here are some examples: "For thou hast cast all my sins behind thy back" (Isaiah 38:17), and "As far as the east is from the west, so far hath he removed our transgressions from us" (Psalm 103:12). And another:

> Who is a God like unto thee, that pardoneth iniquity, and passeth by the transgression of the remnant of his heritage? He retaineth not his anger for ever, because he delighteth in mercy.
>
> He will turn again, he will have compassion upon us; he will subdue our iniquities; and thou wilt cast all their sins into the depths of the sea. (Micah 7:18–19)

The rebellious and sinful ways of Alma, (described in Mosiah 28:4 as "the vilest of sinners") were "taken away" so totally that he became a major prophet and was later described, in Alma 10:7, as "a holy man." Assurances by the Lord, such as "I will also save you from all your uncleanness" (Ezekiel 36:29), and "I am able to make you holy" (D&C 60:7) help us to believe that His role as a perfect Savior will extend to us as well.

> And it shall come to pass, that whoso repenteth and is baptized in my name shall be filled: and if he endureth to the end, behold, *him will I hold guiltless* before my Father at that day when I shall stand to judge the world.
>
> Now this is the commandment: Repent, all ye ends of the earth, and come unto me and be baptized in my name, that ye may be sanctified by the reception of the Holy Ghost, *that ye may stand spotless before me at the last day.*" (3 Nephi 27:16, 20; emphasis added)

In summary, the "intent" of the glad tidings of the Atonement is to bring about "the bowels of mercy" which can then "overpower" and "satisfy the demands of justice." It is to bring about the "means unto men that they may have faith unto repentance" and encircle each repentant person "in the arms of safety" (see Alma 34:15–16).

"And if they know me," said the Lord, "they shall come forth, and shall have a place eternally at my right hand" (Mosiah 26:24). "And all of this," added Alma, so that "ye may at last be brought to sit down with Abraham, Isaac, and Jacob, and the holy prophets who have been ever since the world began, having your garments spotless even as their garments are spotless, in the kingdom of heaven to go no more out" (Alma 7:25).

Elder Curtis pondered what he had read. He reread the last paragraph, and then stood and returned to the president's office with renewed hope and confidence but also with an urgency to find out how to make this happen.

Further Discussion on
the Glad Tidings

*T*he president smiled. "Welcome back, Elder. I guess the main thing I wanted you to learn from your last two articles is that it is not a sign of failure or inferiority to need to repent and ask for forgiveness—it is all part of God's plan for our learning from our mortal experience." He pulled a paper from his forgiveness folder in the resource drawer and remarked, "This is really important to our spiritual health." Handing the paper to the elder, he said, "Here, I'd like you to read this statement from the *Ensign*."

The elder took the paper and read, " 'It is not a sign of weakness to avail ourselves of the Atonement. Rather, it shows courage, faith, and gratitude. The Atonement allows us not only to repent of sin but also to receive an outpouring of the Savior's grace, which strengthens us when we simply do not have the power to overcome our human weaknesses. It allows the Savior to share our burdens and compensate for our many inadequacies' (see Matthew 11:28–30; Ether 12:27)."[1]

"People could have so much more peace in their lives if they could only believe that," President Love said. "But one of the difficulties that many of us have in feeling forgiven after we repent is our cold shoulder expectation."

Elder Curtis asked, "What does that mean?"

"Elder Curtis, surely you've been given the cold shoulder. One of the things the natural man tends to do when they feel someone has hurt them or offended them is to make them pay for a while before allowing reconciliation. This delay is called 'giving them the cold shoulder.' It means that instead of looking for ways to make things right between us, we pull back. Because it is so easy to do this to each other, it is natural for us to expect the Lord to treat us the same way when we sin. Of course we believe that He will eventually forgive us after we repent, but even though we are genuinely sorry and repentant, it is still easy to expect a period of time where we get a cold shoulder, even from Him. Because we did wrong, we now expect the Holy Ghost will be withheld, the answers to our prayers will be delayed, and so forth, because we must be made to pay."

The president continued, "It is foolish to attribute our pettiness to a perfect and loving God, but sometimes we do that anyway. I know I have. In fact, when I heard Elder Hugh W. Pinnock give a talk at BYU, he taught something that bothered me for a long time. I remember the words exactly, because I wrote them down to ponder. He told us that in a previous talk at BYU, he had commented that 'the Lord forgives us in a millionth of a millisecond.' But then he added something even more disturbing. He told us that after saying that, a young man had approached him and said, 'I don't think what you said is right.' And then Elder Pinnock stunned us with his reply to the young man. He stated, 'Well, perhaps I made a mistake—the Savior forgives us instantly. It doesn't even take him a millionth of a millisecond.' "[2]

The president admitted, "That really troubled me because, to me, it made it sound like forgiveness is something cheap and really easy to get. I remembered President Kimball warning that '[sin] is not something that can be set aside with a brushing-off gesture, or even with feigned sorrow, or even with a determination never to repeat the error.' "[3] And I thought about the scripture that says when we obtain forgiveness and then deliberately return to our sinful ways, the former sins will be added back to our accountability (see D&C 82:7). Because President Kimball had been so strict about the importance of sincere repentance and the effort to win forgiveness, I couldn't reconcile that with Elder Pinnock's statement. Look, I put another example of President Kimball's quotes there on your paper."

The elder read, " 'In all our expressions of wonder and gratitude at our Father's loving and forgiving attitude, we must not be misled into supposing either that forgiveness may be considered lightly or that sin may be repeated with impunity after protestations of repentance' "[4]

The president continued, "So I felt confused, because I knew Elder Pinnock could not mean to imply that forgiveness was something cheap or to be had easily with no godly sorrow and true repentance. And I knew that as a member of the Seventy, he must know more about this than I did, and so I began to study. I discovered I'd had no conception of how kind and loving and merciful and *eager* to forgive our Heavenly Father is. I went back through *The Miracle of Forgiveness* and found a couple of statements by President Kimball that seemed to support Elder Pinnock's statement. They are right there on your paper, Elder. Read the first one please."

The elder picked up the paper again and read:

> Every normal individual is responsible for the sins he commits, and would be similarly liable to the punishment attached to those broken laws. However, Christ's death on the cross offers us exemption from the eternal punishment for most sins. He took upon himself the punishment for the sins of all the world, with the understanding that those who repent and come unto him will be forgiven of their sins and freed from the punishment.[5]

The president added, "Look here at the next quote: 'When [a sinner] repents and corrects his life, the Lord will smile and receive him.'[6] I really like that. It makes me feel more welcome. Now, I know those quotes don't talk about the *speed* of His forgiveness, like Elder Pinnock described. But there are many scriptures that do, and they taught me that God is never reluctant or slow to forgive but is always ready, even eager, to forgive. I've put several of them there on your resource paper. You read the first one."

Elder Curtis read: " 'For his anger kindleth against the wicked; they repent, and in a moment it is turned away, and they are in his favor, and he giveth them life; therefore, weeping may endure for a night, but joy cometh in the morning' (JST Psalm 30:5)."

The president took the paper and said, "Moses taught that our Father is a God who is 'keeping mercy for thousands, forgiving iniquity and transgression and sin' (Exodus 34:7). Isaiah addressed the same idea when he admonished, 'Let the wicked forsake his way, and the unrighteous man his thoughts: and let him return unto the Lord, and he will have mercy upon him; and to our God, *for he will abundantly pardon*' (Isaiah 55:7; emphasis added). And the Lord Himself told Alma, 'As often as my people repent will I forgive them their trespasses against me' (Mosiah 26:30)." He added, "My favorite phrase is 'freely forgive' because I can't find the slightest possibility of reluctance or hesitancy in that phrase. See, here it is on your paper: 'For behold, this is my church; whosoever is baptized shall be baptized unto repentance. And whomsoever ye receive shall believe in my name; and him will I *freely forgive*' (Mosiah 26:22; emphasis added).

"As I continued to study, I began reviewing talks by other General Authorities. One of the most comforting and encouraging statements that I found was this one, by J. Reuben Clark. You're too young to remember him, but he was a member of the First Presidency. Here, you read it please."

The elder took back the paper and read: " 'I feel that the Savior will give that punishment which is the very least that our transgressions will justify. And I believe that when it comes to making the rewards for our good conduct, he will give us the maximum that it is possible to give' "[7]

The president said, "Thank you, Elder. Repentance and forgiveness are not detours. They are the most direct path to the celestial kingdom. Here, let's have you read what Elder Boyd K. Packer taught."

The elder read: " 'All that has been printed or preached or sung or built or taught or broadcast has been to the end that men and women and children can know the redeeming influence of the Atonement of Christ in their everyday lives and be at peace.' "[8]

"Now, Elder, I want you to read the next scripture on your paper, and then I want you to explain it to me, because it surely sounds like a contradiction."

Elder Curtis read, " 'He hath not dealt with us after our sins; nor rewarded us according to our iniquities' (Psalm 103:10)."

The president asked, "How can this be? Why doesn't the Lord require us to make full payment for every sin? Why is the Lord's justice tempered with mercy when we repent?"

He did not reply for several moments. His mind raced as he reviewed all that he had been taught that day and then slowly, as if his mouth was not used to expressing such an idea, he answered, "It's because His love is more concerned with saving and exalting us than it is with punishment. And it's because Jesus suffered and died for our sins so that as we repent, He, as our substitute and advocate before justice, can apply mercy and we will not have to suffer the full penalties of the law if we repent and obey."

"Elder, I'm proud of you. That was well said. The Father is not looking on people who repent as tarnished or stained, but as His children who are making progress in returning to Him. And the Savior is not looking upon us with regret or begrudging that He must now go and make an accounting with justice. Instead, He is rejoicing that we are allowing Him to do it so that His suffering on our part will not have been in vain. Now open your Doctrine and Covenants with me and let me teach you how to cross-reference some scriptural passages. Let's go to section fifty-eight. Why don't you read verse forty-two?"

He read: " 'Behold, he who has repented of his sins, the same is forgiven, and I, the Lord, *remember them no more*' (D&C 58:42; emphasis added)." The elder said, "I've heard that before, and I don't get it. Christ is God and He knows everything, so I don't see how He can possibly forget our sins."

The president replied, "But, Elder, He did not say that He *forgets* them. What He said was that He chooses not to remember. Once we put our sins in our past and live a better life of obedience, they are irrelevant to Him. And not focusing on the memory of our repented sins is not just for our benefit, but it is also for His. This is clarified in the Old Testament. That's why I wanted to teach you how to cross-reference these complementary verses so that you can always remind yourself of the full meaning of a doctrine. Here, look at my scripture. I have referenced eight other scriptures in the margins, just for this one verse. One of them is in Isaiah. Let's have you read that."

" 'I, even I, am he that blotteth out thy transgressions *for mine own sake*, and will not remember thy sins' (Isaiah 43:25; emphasis added)."

The president commented, "You see the important addition here? Not only does He not remember the sins He has forgiven, but He releases them from His memory *for His own sake* and so should we. That's why He used the symbolism of blotting them out of the record."

The elder said, "That's another thing that bothers me. The way I understand it, the Day of Judgment is when each of our lives will be reviewed in such detail that every good thing and bad thing we've ever done or said will be there for everyone to see. Like it was being shouted from the rooftops, I think it says somewhere. (See Luke 12:3.) But if all the sins of which we've been previously forgiven are blotted out, it will be so obvious, like the playback is full of censored scenes, or full of bleeps or something. It will be so embarrassing."

"That is exactly how I used to picture it too," replied President Love. "And I had the same concern. Look here at the top of my page. You see that I have a cross-reference to Ezekiel 18 that answers that very question. Give me a minute while you look it up and let me see if I can find a picture to show you that helped me to envision how this is going to work."

The elder fumbled through the Old Testament, trying to find Ezekiel, while the president rummaged through a box of photos. To his delight, President Love found what he was looking for just as the elder found the chapter. He said, "Here, before we read the verse, take a look at this photo that I took on the island of St. Thomas, in the Caribbean.

"The governor put up this campaign sign on one of the busiest roads on the island. But there was something in those last four words that I believe his party considered politically incorrect, so they blotted out the words. When I saw this sign, I thought *That's exactly what it will be like on the Day of Judgment.* Is that how you have been envisioning these 'blotting out' scriptures?"

"Yes!" replied the elder excitedly.

"All right," the president replied, "now let's read verses twenty-one and twenty-two and learn why this sign does *not* represent how the blotting out will look on the Day of Judgment."

" 'But if the wicked will turn from all his sins that he hath committed, and keep all my statutes, and do that which is lawful and right, he shall live, he shall not die. All his transgressions that he hath committed, *they shall not be mentioned unto him*: in his righteousness that he hath done he shall live' (Ezekiel 18:21–22; emphasis added)."

"So," said the president, "do you see how this scripture changed my opinion of how it will be? If the blotted out sins are not even mentioned, then they can't be anything like the sign in that picture. Also, since the Lord has chosen not to remember things that we have repented of and been forgiven for, I can't imagine what purpose would be served by showing all the blotted out parts of our life. Not even mentioned! No telltale blots even showing. That is really encouraging. Here's the way Elder Dallin H. Oaks expressed this idea: 'The Final Judgment is not just an evaluation of a sum total of good and evil acts—what we have done. It is an acknowledgment of the final effect of our acts and thoughts—what we have become.'[9] Now, let's go have supper with the family and then I'll give you something more to study at your bunk this evening."

***

After supper they returned to his office, where the president said, "Now, Elder, so far our studies today have focused on repentance. Actually, there is a lot more to learn about that process, but we will tackle that tomorrow. I think the next thing you need to understand is that repentance is only a beginning—not an end. You must understand that no matter how sincere your repentance might be, no matter how complete you think it is, no matter how totally it might change your outward behavior patterns and obedience, it will never change your inner nature or give you the 'born again' experience which will make you a new creature in Christ."

He continued, "The initial part of repentance, the stopping of sin and turning to the Lord, is but a preliminary step to what we really need, and that is the change of heart and change of nature that allows us to receive divine healing. The Lord reminded us of this multi-step process when He invited, 'Return unto me, and repent of your sins, and be converted, *that I may heal you*' (3 Nephi 9:13; emphasis added). It is through this lifelong process of repentance, increasing conversion and receiving divine healing that we can eventually be born again and receive the mighty change of heart and nature.

"I know my son invited you to go jogging with him this evening, and that's fine with me as long as you study this article before we start again in the morning. Do you have any questions?"

"No."

"All right then, we'll resume in the morning."

NOTES

1   Brent L. Top, "A Balanced Life," *Ensign*, Apr. 2005, 29.

2   "Necessities of Living," *BYU Devotional Speeches of The Year*, 29 May 1979, 120.

3   *The Miracle of Forgiveness*, 154.

4   "God Will Forgive," *Ensign*, Mar. 1982, 7.

5   *The Miracle of Forgiveness*, 133.

6   Ibid., 89.

7   "As Ye Sow," *BYU Devotional Speeches of the Year*, 1955, 7.

8   "The Touch of the Master's Hand," *Ensign*, May 2001, 24.

9   "The Challenge to Become," *Ensign*, Nov. 2000, 32.

A Challenging Run

*A*fter Elder Curtis changed clothes in preparation for the run, he laid down on the bunk, thinking about the day and feeling amazed by the love and support he had received from the President. After a day of confronting issues and climbing intense and unfamiliar doctrinal mountains, he looked forward to a relaxing run on level ground. When Jeff didn't come as soon as he had expected, he sat on the bunk and began to read his assignment.

Reaching Beyond Repentance

Alma testified that Christ "has all power to save every man that believeth on his name and *bringeth forth* fruit meet for repentance" (Alma 12:15; emphasis added). It is the "bringing forth" of spiritual growth toward the second birth that elevates repentance beyond the mere abandonment (or forsaking) of sin.

It is true that in the beginning phase of repentance we focus on "turning away" from our sins as we stop doing whatever was wrong. But true repentance, the repentance that will lead us into eternal life, is much more than stepping on the brakes of a bad habit. Alma testified that Christ "has all power to save every man that believeth on his name and *bringeth forth* fruit meet for repentance" (Alma

12:15; emphasis added). It is the "bringing forth" of spiritual growth toward the second birth that elevates repentance beyond the mere abandonment (or forsaking) of sin. As Elder Dallin H. Oaks taught:

Just as Elder Curtis was getting interested, the president's oldest son stepped in and announced that it was time to go. The elder didn't mind a bit. Actually, he was glad for the change. He knew there was more study to do when he got back, but for now, he set the paper aside. It was going to feel really good to give his mind a rest.

As they ran, he chatted freely with Jeff, who politely avoided discussing the elder's day with his father. A tall, lanky boy with black hair, Jeff would soon be submitting papers for his own mission. For a fleeting moment, Elder Curtis considered giving him some advice about being honest, but he quickly dismissed the thought. They ran for about thirty minutes, working up a good sweat. It felt good, and they both looked forward to a shower and another glass of the delicious lemonade they had enjoyed at supper.

Shortly after they turned back toward the mission home, they saw two elders walking on the sidewalk. Instinctively, they stopped to say hello. It quickly proved to be a big mistake.

After the initial exchange of hellos, one of them asked, "Hey, Elder Curtis, we've been calling your apartment all day to arrange those splits that Elder Jones asked for. How come we never got an answer?"

"Well," Elder Curtis began, hesitant about what to say.

"Where have you guys been all day?" he continued. "And by the way, how come you're here with Jeff and not out teaching? What's going on?" he asked inquisitively. "Where is your companion?"

Elder Curtis had not anticipated the rapid-fire questioning. He didn't want others to know how intensely he was counseling with the president. And he certainly didn't want people speculating about whether he might be sent home or, worse yet, wondering why. As his mind raced to find an answer, his fear grew that anything he said might create rumors that could spread throughout the mission. Unexpectedly, he suddenly found himself crippled once again by the fear of others' opinions. His heart sunk as he continued to hesitate, unsure of what to say.

Before he could think of a reply, Jeff volunteered that Elder Jones had been out training Elders Rich and Elder Johnson all day. But that explanation left Elder Curtis's time unaccounted for. Not even suspecting a secret, the elder asked, teasingly, "So, Elder Curtis, does that mean you got to play with Jeff all day, or have you been hanging out with the president?"

The question was innocent enough, but when they saw the deep blush and look of panic on Elder Curtis's face, they immediately sensed there was something he did not want them to know.

Sensing the fear in Elder Curtis, and without time to weigh what he said, Jeff blurted, "Look guys, he's taking Elder Brown's place in the office. And no, he didn't 'hang out' with the president all day. They just had a few talks, so cut us some slack, okay?"

Never dreaming just how right he was, the elder continued the teasing. Raising his eyebrows in mock astonishment, the elder asked innocently, "Hey, you're not one of the president's 'projects,' are you?"

His companion joined in on what he thought was just innocent fun. "Come on, Curtis, we're all part of the same team here. You can tell us. What did you do to get into such trouble? Did you meet a girl? Or was it something back home? Come on, man, tell us what's going on."

About to drop it and get on to their appointment, they suddenly sobered as they could see from the pain in Elder Curtis's face that he actually was hiding something dreadful. Suddenly there was a deathly silence as they regretted what they had done. But before they could think how to apologize, Jeff grabbed Elder Curtis by the arm and said, "Come on, Elder, let's go." Grateful for an escape, he spun and followed Jeff's lead.

With his mind spinning in unresolved fears, he imagined the worst. *They're going to tell everyone,* he thought. *Now everyone in the mission is going to be wondering what I did, and the rumors will be flying.* As they continued running, he soon convinced himself: *I bet people will be taking bets on when I go home.*

Feeling that he had to say something, Jeff apologized, "Hey, Elder, I'm sorry for what I said. Whatever is going on in your personal life, you're lucky to have so much time with Dad. He'll help you straighten things out. I'm sure they didn't mean to embarrass you."

Elder Curtis muttered a thanks, but in his panic and fear, he felt like just like he did when he was back home, facing interviews where he mistakenly thought his sins would be exposed and people would look down on him when they discovered the truth about his past. Though his fears were probably groundless, his confused mind reasoned, *There is no way they aren't going to spread this around. And then, even if the president lets me stay, people will never leave it alone until they find out what my problem is. I'm doomed either way.*

When they arrived back at the mission home, Jeff went upstairs to shower, but Elder Curtis went right to the president's office. He was disappointed to find it empty. Then he looked to see if, by any luck, Sister Richardson might still be there. That was rather ridiculous, because it was now past eight o'clock. But, by chance, she had actually come back after supper to do some printing for zone conferences.

She saw instantly that something was wrong. Before she could inquire, Elder Curtis, with a trembling voice, pleaded, "Sister Richardson, please, I've got to talk to the president right now."

She said, "I'm sorry, Elder, but that's impossible. He had to go to a meeting quite some distance from here. I don't expect he'll be back before midnight."

His heart sank, and with no prodding from her, he spilled out the story of their encounter and all his fears.

She hugged him and advised, soothingly, "Elder, I'm sure they meant no harm. Don't let what they said bother you. This is the time you've got to be strong and stick to the task."

Still convinced of the worst, he groaned, "It's no use. I'll never live this down. There's no way out of this. I'm doomed whether I stay here or go home. I should never have come on this mission. I don't fit in anywhere."

"Now listen to that devil putting words in your mouth." Putting her hands on her hips, she admonished sternly, "You listen to me, Elder. If I were your mother I'd have you standing in the corner for whining like that. You've got to get a grip or you're going to make things worse for yourself. Whatever it is that's going on in your life, you've got more important things to worry about right now than rumors and gossip.

"Now, you go on up to bed and the president will help you straighten this all out tomorrow. You remember that he loves you, and the Lord loves you. And I love you too," she added, giving him a push out the door.

She left a note on the president's desk, explaining the situation. Then she left for the evening.

Reaching Beyond Repentance

*E*lder Curtis paced the bedroom for an hour, worrying about his imagined rumors and loss of reputation. Then he plopped on the bunk, but he could not get to sleep. Finally, he guessed he might as well study his assignment. He got up, turned on a lamp, sat in the easy chair, and started back at the beginning. As he reread the first two paragraphs, he realized he had no recollection of what they said. He needed to pay better attention.

Reaching Beyond Repentance

Alma testified that Christ "has all power to save every man that believeth on his name and *bringeth forth* fruit meet for repentance" (Alma 12:15; emphasis added). It is the "bringing forth" of spiritual growth toward the second birth that elevates repentance beyond the mere abandonment (or forsaking) of sin.

It is true that in the beginning phase of repentance we focus on "turning away" from our sins as we stop doing whatever was wrong. But true repentance, the repentance that will lead us into eternal life, is much more than stepping on the brakes of a bad habit. Alma testified that Christ "has all power to save every man that believeth on his name and *bringeth forth* fruit meet for repentance" (Alma 12:15; emphasis added). It is the "bringing forth" of spiritual growth toward the second birth that elevates repentance beyond the mere abandonment (or forsaking) of sin. As Elder Dallin H. Oaks taught:

> We tend to think of the results of repentance as simply cleansing us from sin. But that is an incomplete view of the matter. A person who sins is like a tree that bends easily in the wind. On a windy and rainy day, the tree bends so deeply against the ground that the leaves become soiled with mud, like sin. If we focus only on cleaning the leaves, the weakness in the tree that allowed it to bend and soil its leaves may remain. Similarly, a person who is merely sorry to be soiled by sin will sin again in the next high wind. The susceptibility to repetition continues until the tree has been strengthened. . . .
>
> That strengthening is essential for us to realize the purpose of the cleansing, which is to return to our Heavenly Father. To be admitted to his presence, we must be more than clean. We must also be changed from a morally weak person who has sinned into a strong person with the spiritual stature to dwell in the presence of God. ("Sin and Suffering," *Ensign*, Jul. 1992, 70)

Often we come to God in what we think is repentance, but seek only release of the pain of shame. We pray about *symptoms*, rather than about becoming whole, seeking *relief* rather than *healing* and a change of nature. For example: "Please help me stop smoking, drinking, doing drugs, or pornography. Please help me to stop cussing. Help me with my temper. Help me to stop yelling at my kids." Certainly these are righteous desires and represent the surface kinds of imperfections that we should be striving to overcome. But they are only *symptoms*, symptoms of the spiritual bankruptcy that infects every natural man and woman who needs to be born again.

Christian author C. S. Lewis wrote, "It may be hard for an egg to turn into a bird: it would be a jolly sight harder for it to learn to fly while remaining an egg. We are like eggs at present. And you cannot go on indefinitely being just an ordinary, decent egg. We must be hatched or go bad" (*Mere Christianity*, 169–70). It is difficult to *stop* doing something because that is negative. Positive action is easier to initiate than negative reaction. Nature hates a vacuum. The sin of which we need to repent should be replaced with good performance or it will leave a hole in our behavior patterns that further temptations and former bad habits will fill with their downward pull. We promote progress and spiritual growth when we focus on forward motion. Therefore, to break a bad habit or conquer a sin, a focus on positive things which will bring us to Christ is better than a focus on things we choose no longer to do.

However, our repentance alone can only satisfy the *beginnings* of the law. We need Christ to change us in a way that will satisfy the *ends* of the law and put a divine stamp of approval on our repentance. "Behold, he offereth himself a sacrifice for sin, to answer the ends of the law, unto all those who have a broken heart and a contrite spirit; and unto none else can the ends of the law be answered" (2 Nephi 2:7). In order for Christ to satisfy the demands of justice and "answer the ends of the law" on our behalf, we must do more than repent. We must be born again.

Scriptures that discuss the concept of being born again present it as a spiritual *necessity*, not a suggestion. For example, Jesus proclaimed that "except a man be born again, he cannot see the kingdom of God" and then counseled his confused audience, "Marvel not that I said unto thee, Ye must be born again" (John 3:3, 7). Alma emphasized the same theme: "I say unto you the aged, and also the middle aged, and the rising generation . . . that they must repent and be born again" (Alma 5:49).

Paul emphasized the "born again" experience when he stated, "if any man be in Christ, he [becomes] a new creature: old things are passed away; behold all things are become new" (2 Corinthians 5:17). He also emphasized our need to be changed by the Spirit through the process of ongoing repentance when he stressed our need to "put off the old man with his deeds" (Colossians 3:9), and that we "put on the new man, which after God is created in righteousness and true holiness" (Ephesians 4:24).

Fidgeting in the chair, Elder Curtis lamented how distant this all seemed for him. What chance did he have of ever becoming a new creature or feeling clean before the Lord? All he could think about was how his life seemed to be falling apart. He had no stomach for continuing. But, after pacing for a while, listening in vain for the president's return, he grudgingly continued.

The Book of Mormon explains such statements to mean being "*changed* from their carnal and fallen state, to a state of righteousness, being redeemed of God, becoming his sons and daughters; And *thus they become new creatures*; and unless they do this, they can in nowise inherit the kingdom of God" (Mosiah 27:25–26; emphasis added). It is this lifelong process of being "hatched," or transformed from the fallen, natural-man state, that is the moving forward, growing and progressing, or "bringing forth" part of repentance.

This process is not so much about what we drive out of ourselves as it is about what we fill ourselves with. It is in reaching for this full repentance that we move past the mere restraint of inappropriate behavior into the "born again" process. That is because no matter how valiant and sincere we are, no matter how earnestly we try; *no one* can change their carnal nature by their own repentance alone, for as President Ezra Taft Benson explained: "The Lord works from the inside out. The world works from the outside in. The world would shape human behavior, but Christ can change human nature" ("Born of God," *Ensign*, Nov. 1985, 6). When we only pray about our outward behavioral symptoms it is like we are trying to remain as eggs. Better eggs, yes, but not *transformed* eggs.

Real repentance, then, means striving to be fully acceptable to Him, not just to feel good because we put one unworthy thing out of our life. So, as we move past the preparatory stopping and turning phase of our initial repentance, the fulfillment phase focuses on moving forward toward Christ's promise of being born again and receiving the mighty change of heart that lifts us above our fallen natures.

That's what I want, Elder Curtis thought, *to really feel acceptable.* He felt the urge that this would be a good time to have a real prayer, but he felt drowsy, and since he was almost done reading the article, he continued.

And with full and continuing repentance, our hope and confidence is that as we receive the spiritual rebirth and transformation into His image, "we [will] know that, when he shall appear, we shall be like him" (1 John 3:2; Moroni 7:48). What does that promise to be "like him" actually mean? Moroni defined it as being sanctified and made "holy, without spot."

> Yea, come unto Christ, and be perfected in him, and deny yourselves of all ungodliness; and if ye shall deny yourselves of all ungodliness, and love God with all your might, mind and strength, then is his grace sufficient for you, that by his grace ye may be perfect in Christ; and if by the grace of God ye are perfect in Christ, ye can in nowise deny the power of God.
>
> And again, if ye by the grace of God are perfect in Christ, and deny not his power, then are ye sanctified in Christ by the grace of God, through the shedding of the blood of Christ, which is in the covenant of the Father unto the remission of your sins, that ye become holy, without spot. (Moroni 10:32–33)

Other prophets have expanded on the blessings that follow full repentance and change of nature. For example, Peter pointed out that there "are given unto us exceeding great and precious promises" (2 Peter 1:4) through the gospel, the Atonement of Christ, and the assurance of spiritual rebirth. These promises teach us that through Christ, we can overcome our fallen, carnal nature and become new, worthy and acceptable in His sight, and also "that we may be purified even as he is pure" (Moroni 7:48), becoming "pure and spotless before God" (Alma 13:12), even "partakers of his holiness" (Hebrews 12:10), and *"partakers of the divine nature,* having escaped the corruption that is in the world through lust" (2 Peter 1:4; emphasis added).

He finally fell asleep in the chair, filled with misgivings more than with hope, and completely unaware of the encouragement and hope that would fill his life the next day.

I've Got to Go Home—Today!

At six thirty the next morning, when the president and his family came downstairs for family scriptures and breakfast, they found Elder Curtis pacing in the living room. The moment he saw them he exclaimed, "President, I have to talk to you!"

"Elder Curtis, I can see that you're upset, but we can't talk now. I have family duties to attend to first. Why don't you get your Bible so that you can join us."

"But, President . . ."

"No buts, Elder. We'll talk after breakfast. Now hurry up. We have kids to get off to school."

Reluctantly Elder Curtis went downstairs to his cubicle and returned with his scriptures.

After the family had completed their scripture study and breakfast, Elder Curtis and President Love went downstairs to his office where the elder explained his growing concern about the embarrassment he feared would be caused by the two elders from last night. He insisted that he probably should just go home and face the consequences there.

The president replied, "Elder Curtis, I can understand your fear. I'm sorry for your additional concern, but I am surprised that after all we discussed yesterday, you could still think that running away is the thing to do. I wish you would understand that the only opinion about you that really matters is that of your Heavenly Father and your Savior."

He continued, "I'm telling you again that I want you to stay until we both know what is the right thing to do. Whether you stay to finish your mission or go home to square things with your priesthood leaders and family, it should be because that is the best course of action for your spiritual welfare. It certainly should not be decided by fear or embarrassment over someone's opinion. That's what put you into this predicament in the first place. Will you agree to this?"

Elder Curtis hung his head in resignation and mumbled a yes.

Sensing the need for a change of scene, the president stood and suggested, "Listen, it's a beautiful morning. Let's go talk in the backyard." The grounds of the mission home were large, and there was plenty of room to walk in the beautifully landscaped yard.

Once they were alone outside, the president said, "I want to tell you a story. At the end of a trip we took for our anniversary, when it was time to fly home, my wife and I went to the airport very early in the morning. There was hardly anyone there, so I was surprised that the ticket lady was so busy at her computer. I don't know what was so important, but she was typing furiously on her keyboard and never even looked up to acknowledge our presence. But she did ask, as she continued typing, 'Final destination?' I winked at my wife and said, 'Heaven.' The typing stopped and she looked up at us with a big grin. We became instant friends and I think she probably had a better day. I know I did."

Elder Curtis chuckled. The president observed, "Yes, it is amusing, but it has a point that can help you. Yesterday you came to me because you wanted to find a way out of the pain of your unresolved guilt. That was good. You were sincere and you had good intentions, but your goal was incomplete. I don't blame you for wanting to find a way out of your pain; that is the right thing to do. But if that is all you set as your goal, or your final destination, you will be cheating yourself and your future posterity.

"As we continue studying together, you are going to raise your sights a bit, as you learn how to properly repent of your situation. That will also be an important and a good direction. But again, if that is as high as you set your final destination, you may miss the most important goal of all: becoming like Christ and obtaining eternal life with Him in the celestial kingdom."

Elder Curtis groaned, "I see your point, but you set the bar so high. I feel like I can't even get myself past the basics and you want me to reach for a 'born again' experience. I'm so deep in the hole I don't see how I'll ever get out."

"Elder, sometimes, the deeper the hole, the easier it is to reach for the Savior's help. Let's go back in the office because I want you to read something that helps me when I feel like I'm in one of those holes."

As they turned back toward the house, the elder protested incredulously, "President, I can't imagine you being in a hole!"

The president smiled and put his arm around him as they entered the house. "Elder, I've been in many holes in my life. Right now, you've got me down in the bottom of *your* hole." When they reached the office, he pulled out a paper and read to the elder:

> We think we must climb to a certain height of goodness before we can reach God. But He says not 'at the end of the way you may find me;' He says 'I am the way; I am the road under your feet, the road that begins just as low down as you happen to be.'
>
> If we are in a hole then the Way begins in the hole. The moment we set our face in the same direction as His, we are walking with God.[1]

"So, Elder, I am going to give you some time to make your decision and then . . ."

He interrupted, "President, I don't need any time. I've already made my decision. There is really only one decision that makes sense. But I'm still in that hole and I still don't understand how to get out of it. You told me yesterday that we had a lot more to learn about repentance. Perhaps that will help me. Can we finish that up today?"

"Yes, I believe we can. You have a quick mind and you will find that what we study today is going to give you a better sense of direction and explanation of what you need to do. But it won't be as simple as an A-B-C checklist or a step-by-step guide. I think it is human nature to want something like that by which to measure our progress. But it is gratifying to me to recognize that *we* don't need to understand the process of the second birth as much as to trust and accept that *Christ* understands it.

"For example, when we need light to eliminate darkness from our homes, we simply flip the light switch. Receiving that light does not depend upon our knowing and understanding all the complexities of generating and delivering electricity to our home. We just trust the process to work. Taking advantage of Christ's Atonement and His power to change our desires and our fallen nature can work the same way, because He knows exactly what needs to be done.

"Elder, each individual comes to the Savior with different sins, weaknesses, backgrounds, hang-ups, and needs. That's why the change-of-heart part of the Atonement takes place one person at a time, just as it will for you. The Savior has the perfect knowledge and wisdom to give each person individual, *customized* tutoring, as well as the grace and power to help us rise above the darkness of carnality into the light, joy, peace and victory of being born again.

"I know you feel uncertain right now, because you know you are going to have to depend upon something you cannot itemize or control. But when you learn to do your part, you can be confident that the Savior will do His. And I think you will find it an exciting adventure to humbly accept His divine caring for you and to simply let go and let God be in charge.

"We haven't discussed obedience and keeping our covenants yet, and we need to do that. You remember we learned that real repentance means more than just stopping something bad. It means moving forward with obedience and forming new and better habits. However, before we do that, there is something else that comes first, and that is learning to make proper decisions—as you have done this morning.

"If we can't train ourselves to respond to our conscience with a positive decision, then we'll never get to the other principles of repentance. As disciples of Christ, we must train ourselves to decide to decide. Elder Joseph B. Wirthlin pointed out that one consequence of procrastination is that 'it clutters our minds with unfinished business and makes us uneasy.'[2] That state of mind is not helpful. If making a change in our lives would be the right thing to do, doing it *now* will always be better than taking a chance on later.

"Now you go to your cubicle for a few minutes and get your thoughts together while I take care of some phone calls, or Sister Richardson will have my hide. While you're there, you can study this brief article on procrastination. Then you can come back and we'll get to work."

NOTES

1 Helen Wodehouse, as quoted in *Prayer Can Change Your Life*, 244–45.

2 "The Message: It Starts in the Heart," *Ensign*, Feb. 2005, 6.

Choosing to Choose

*E*lder Curtis felt some encouragement. He sat at the desk and began to read with new enthusiasm.

Choosing to Choose

When Adam and Eve left the Garden of Eden, "there was a space granted unto man in which he might repent; therefore this life became a probationary state; a time to prepare to meet God" (Alma 12:24). This "space" of time is called mortal probation. One of the most important aspects of mortal probation is the agency we have to choose between good and evil. "Therefore, cheer up your hearts, and remember that ye are free to act for yourselves—to choose the way of everlasting death or the way of eternal life" (2 Nephi 10:23).

We are not only *free* to choose, but when our conscience taps us on the shoulder, we have an *obligation* to choose. Every choice we make leads us either *upward*, toward greater spirituality, freedom and self-mastery, or *downward*, toward enslavement and sorrow. The character that develops within us from the accumulation of these daily choices determines whether our mortal probation results in an eternal reward of joy in the celestial kingdom or a lesser reward in a lower kingdom.

This obligation of choice has thundered through centuries of scripture. For example, we have Joshua's powerful words: "Choose you this day whom ye will serve" (Joshua 24:15). Moroni counseled, "Be wise in the days of your probation" (Mormon 9:28). And Jacob warned, "Wo unto him that has the law given, yea, that has all the commandments of God, like unto us, and that transgresseth them, and that wasteth the days of his probation, for awful is his state!" (2 Nephi 9:27). The Lord told us a lot about the importance and urgency of this mortal probation when He cautioned, "For if you will that I give unto you a place in the celestial world, you must prepare yourselves by doing the things which I have commanded you and required of you" (D&C 78:7). Therefore, "If ye believe me, ye will [choose and] labor while it is called today" (D&C 64:25).

Putting off a choice *is* a choice. It is a choice of procrastination—one of the greatest dangers to our eternal progression. The inclination to procrastinate comes partly because of our fallen nature and partly because of Satan's influence. As President Spencer W. Kimball cautioned, "One of the most serious human defects in all ages is procrastination, an unwillingness to accept personal responsibilities *now*. There are even many members of the Church who are lax and careless and who continually procrastinate. They live the gospel casually but not devoutly" (*The Miracle of Forgiveness*, 7; emphasis in original). That was his description of the "natural man" inclination. He also warned that "[our enemy] delights in procrastination and uses it much. If he cannot convince people to ignore these important matters . . . he will use the strategy of procrastination on the basis that it will achieve his ends eventually" (*The Miracle of Forgiveness*, 246). Similarly, Henry B. Eyring taught:

> And so Satan tempts with procrastination throughout our days of probation. Any choice to delay repentance gives him the chance to steal happiness from one of the spirit children of our Heavenly Father.
>
> We have all been tempted with that delay. . . . He has tempted you and me, and those we love, with thoughts like this: "God is so loving; surely He won't hold me personally responsible for mistakes which are simply the result of being human." And then, if that fails, there is the thought that will almost surely come: "Well, I may be responsible to repent, but this is not a good time to start. If I wait, later will be better." ("Do Not Delay," *Ensign*, Nov. 1999, 34)

Elder curtis paused to regret that he had waited six months to come to the president. *I'll never make that kind of mistake again,* he vowed to himself.

Though we may attempt it, there is no such thing as "casual" repentance. Such an approach is not acceptable to the Lord. To win forgiveness, our repentance must be deep and sincere, and offered with real intent—not something taken lightly. Moroni warned that a person who prays or offers a gift to the Lord, "except he shall do it with real intent it profiteth him nothing" (Moroni 7:6). Surely the same principle would apply to the motives behind our repentance, for we are counseled that when we come to Him, we should "repent, and come with full purpose of heart" (Jacob 6:5), and "offer your whole souls as an offering unto him" (Omni 1:26). A disciple with real intent would never try to escape accountability through procrastination or indifference. In fact, Elder David B. Haight advised, "If we could feel or were sensitive even in the slightest to the matchless love of our Savior and his willingness to suffer for our individual sins, we would cease procrastination and 'clean the slate,' and repent of all our transgressions" ("Our Lord and Savior," *Ensign,* May 1988, 23).

We cannot avoid the consequences of sin by delaying our choice to repent, for if "ye have sinned against the Lord: [you may] be sure [that] your sin will find you out" (Numbers 32:23). "And their transgressions will I bring down with sorrow upon their own heads" (Enos 1:10). This realization adds great meaning to Amulek's teaching on procrastination. "I beseech of you that ye do not procrastinate the day of your repentance until the end; for after this day of life, which is given us to prepare for eternity, behold, if we do not improve our time while in this life, then cometh the night of darkness wherein there can be no labor performed" (Alma 34:33).

Rather than looking for excuses to delay, Alma counseled, "Behold ye must prepare quickly," (Alma 5:28) and a popular hymn reminds us that we never know just how much time we will have to repent, for "The time is far spent; there is little remaining" (*Hymns,* 266). President Spencer W. Kimball warned that "the longer repentance is pushed into the background the more exquisite will be the punishment when it finally comes to the fore" (*The Miracle of Forgiveness,* 141–42). "Oh," he lamented, "If men would only let their sins trouble them early when the sins are small and few, how much anguish would be saved them" (*The Miracle of Forgiveness,* 142).

Elder Curtis looked up as he considered how much better his life would have been if he had taken care of all this back home when he was preparing for his mission. He continued reading.

> These statements remind us of Amulek's warning to those who would choose the lesser path of procrastination: "Ye cannot say, when ye are brought to that awful crisis, that I will repent, that I will return to my God. Nay, ye cannot say this; for that same spirit which doth possess your bodies at the time that ye go out of this life, that same spirit will have power to possess your body in that eternal world" (Alma 34:34).
>
> To help us avoid the temptation of procrastination, the scriptures provide a clear description of the fate of those who choose that lesser way, pass through the veil, and realize that "the harvest [has] ended, and [their] souls [are] not saved" (D&C 45:2). "And, in fine, wo unto all those who die in their sins; for they shall return to God, and behold his face, and remain in their sins" (2 Nephi 9:38). If we allow that to happen, then "[our] days of probation are past; [we] have procrastinated the day of [our] salvation until it is everlastingly too late, and [our] destruction is made sure" (Helaman 13:38). This means that "if ye have procrastinated the day of your repentance even until death, behold, ye have become subjected to the spirit of the devil, and he doth seal you his; therefore, the Spirit of the Lord hath withdrawn from you, and hath no place in you, and the devil hath all power over you; and this is the final state of the [unrepentant] wicked" (Alma 34:35). This will cause them to weep and to wail and to lament: "O that I had repented. O that we had remembered the Lord our God" (Helaman 13:33). How grateful we are for the glad tidings and promise that "as oft as they repented and sought forgiveness, with real intent, they were forgiven" (Moroni 6:8).

Elder Curtis returned to the president's office, anxious to learn what more was needed, anxious to get the process in gear.

Moving into the Process

*W*hen Elder Curtis returned, the president said, "Welcome back, Elder. Do you have any questions about procrastination?"

"No, I don't. I'm ready to get to work."

"Then let's get started, because today we are going into high gear. Before we start the next discussion, I want to summarize your last topic by saying that the issue every person faces with procrastination is not one of simply choosing between sin and repentance but, rather, one of choosing where he wishes to spend eternity. Choosing to repent now can lead to everlasting joy with our loved ones in the presence of Jesus Christ and Heavenly Father, whereas choosing to delay and 'risk one more offense against your God' (see Alma 41:9) can lead to an everlasting life in darkness and misery with the devil.

"That's why the Lord gave priesthood leaders two conclusive tests by which they can evaluate and judge a person's genuine and sincere repentance. He stated, 'By this ye may know if a man repenteth of his sins—behold, he will *confess* them and *forsake* them' (D&C 58:43; emphasis added). You probably remember that we mentioned this verse briefly yesterday. Now it is time to look at it in more depth. We are going to skip the confession part for now and focus on the forsaking part.

"Now, you may think that forcing yourself to abstain from pornography for six months was a pretty good job at forsaking that sin." He turned to his resource drawer and pulled out another lesson. As he handed it to the elder, he said, "Elder Curtis, that was a wonderful beginning, but I want you to study this and see if it might expand your view to more of the healing process than merely restraining or stopping something bad. Not only must we let go of, or abandon our specific sin, but also all our emotional attachments to it." He paused for a moment and then reflected, "Well, I'd better not get into that right now.

"Before you go, I want you to be aware that the Lord taught that in addition to the forsaking part of repentance, there is a cleaving part. This comes as we learn to let go of the bad things and reach for the better. Here are some quick examples. 'And I give unto you a commandment, that ye shall forsake all evil and cleave unto all good' (D&C 98:11). There are lots of other things the scriptures tell us to cleave or hold onto besides the good. For example, we should cling or hold fast to the iron rod, which is the word of God (see 1 Nephi 8:24; 15:24). I think the two most important would be the commands to 'cleave unto the covenants which thou hast made' (D&C 25:13), and 'cleave unto God as he cleaveth unto you' (Jacob 6:5). It really encourages me to know that Heavenly Father is clinging to me even as I repent. You go ahead to your studies now, and come back when you're done."

As the elder left, the president went upstairs to visit with his wife for a moment, hoping he could make it up the stairs before Sister Richardson discovered he was free.

Forsaking Our Sins

inding him available, Sister Richardson kept the elder busy with some office work for about half an hour. Then he went to his cubicle and began to read with expectation.

Forsaking Our Sins

Amulek taught the important repentance doctrine that: "The Lord surely should come to redeem his people, but that he should not come to redeem them *in* their sins, but to redeem them *from* their sins" (Helaman 5:10; emphasis added). Therefore, the forsaking part of repentance includes learning to "abhor that which is evil [and] cleave to that which is good" (Romans 12:9).

A synonym of forsake is to abandon. It not only means to stop doing something but also to stop clinging to or longing for the pleasures of the abandoned sin. When we are truly repentant, those sins that once held us prisoners will become abhorrent to us instead of enticing us with their deceptive lures.

President Spencer W. Kimball had a lot to say about the forsaking part of repentance. One of the key things he stressed was that we must not only forsake the sin itself but also all of the contributing people or factors that pulled us into the sin. For example, "The repenting one must avoid every person, place, thing, or situation which could bring reminders of the sordid past" (*The Miracle of Forgiveness*, 87). And, "In the process of abandoning a sin, it is often necessary to abandon persons, places, things, and situations that are associated with the transgression. This is fundamental. Substitution of a good environment for a bad can hedge the way between the repenting person and his past sin" ("The Gospel of Repentance," *Ensign*, Oct. 1982, 4). His most specific instructions on this principle give good guidance as to just how detailed our "forsaking" must be:

> In abandoning sin one cannot merely wish for better conditions. He must make them. He may need to come to hate the spotted garments and loathe the sin. He must be certain not only that he has abandoned the sin but that he has changed the situations surrounding the sin. He should avoid the places and conditions and circumstances where the sin occurred, for these could most readily breed it again. He must abandon the people with whom the sin was committed. He may not hate the persons involved but he must avoid them and everything associated with the sin.
>
> He must dispose of all letters, trinkets, and things which will remind him of the "old days" and the "old times." He must forget addresses, telephone numbers, people, places and situations from the sinful past, and build a new life. He must eliminate anything which would stir the old memories. (*The Miracle of Forgiveness*, 171–172)

Trying to repent of a sin while clinging to the memories of previous people, places, pleasures, or feelings is something like trying to stand with each foot in a different boat. We cannot expect to grow closer to our Father in Heaven in one area of our lives while clinging to secret sins or memories in other parts. A person, for example, who stops committing *physical* adultery while continuing in *mental* imaginings and longing for an abandoned partner has not truly repented, even though the physical act is being avoided. As President Kimball taught, "The true spirit of repentance, which all should exhibit, embraces a desire to stay away from sin. One cannot simultaneously be repentant and flirt with transgression" (*The Miracle of Forgiveness*, 214). He also said that simply having a desire, intent, or resolve to change is not sufficient. There must be obedience. "The saving power does not extend to him who merely *wants* to change his life. True repentance prods one to action" (*The Miracle of Forgiveness*, 163; emphasis in original).

The action to which he refers is obedience. Elder Bruce R. McConkie taught that "obedience is the first law of heaven, the cornerstone upon which all righteousness and progression rest" (*Mormon Doctrine*, 539). And so the forsaking part of repentance must always expand into obedience. It is for that very reason that we came to this earth. "And we will prove them herewith, to see if they will do all things whatsoever the Lord their God shall command them" (Abraham 3:25).

We all know that obedience does not come natural to fallen mankind. Because of our carnal nature and pride, we must often be chastened and tutored before we learn that Father truly does know what is best for us. We are so blessed that Heavenly Father loves us enough to provide that personal tutoring for each one of us. "And Zion cannot be built up unless it is by the principles of the law of the celestial kingdom; otherwise I cannot receive her unto myself.

"And my people must needs be chastened until they learn obedience, if it must needs be, by the things which they suffer" (D&C 105:5–6).

As a person moves from forsaking to obeying, the abandoned sin may leave huge holes in their life behaviorally, emotionally, and in the way they used to occupy their time. Therefore, an important part of the effort to obey must focus on filling those holes. The scriptural principle "Be not overcome of evil, but overcome evil with good" (Romans 12:21) is explained by President Kimball: "Very frequently people think they have repented and are worthy of forgiveness when all they have done is to express sorrow or regret at the unfortunate happening, but their repentance is barely started. Until they have begun to make changes in their lives, transformation in their habits, and to add new thoughts to their minds, to be sorry is only a bare beginning (Spencer W. Kimball, "What Is True Repentance?" *New Era*, May 1974, 4). Elder Boyd K. Packer provides good counsel on the replacement part of repentance.

> Do not try merely to discard a bad habit or a bad thought. Replace it. When you try to eliminate a bad habit, if the spot where it used to be is left open it will sneak back and crawl again into that empty space. It grew there; it will struggle to stay there. When you discard it, fill up the spot where it was. Replace it with something good. Replace it with unselfish thoughts, with unselfish acts.
>
> Then, if an evil habit or addiction tries to return, it will have to fight for attention. Sometimes it may win. Bad thoughts often have to be evicted a hundred times, or a thousand. But if they have to be evicted ten thousand times, never surrender to them. You are in charge of you.

I repeat, it is very, very difficult to eliminate a bad habit just by trying to discard it. Replace it.

Read in Matthew 12, verses forty-three to forty-five, the parable of the empty house. There is a message in it for you. ("To The One," *BYU Devotional Speeches of the Year*, 21 Feb. 1978, 39)

The errors he had made continued to pile up in the elder's mind, but instead of increasing his discouragement, he was beginning to feel encouraged with some hope of working his way through true repentance. Elder Packer's counsel reminded him of a scripture he had not previously understood. He searched awhile and then found it in Paul's writings. It said, "Be not overcome of evil, but overcome evil with good" (Romans 12:21). Moving forward with positive things instead of merely trying to stop something bad—it made a lot more sense to him now. He found the president waiting for him.

Further Discussion on
Forsaking Our Sins

ow that you can see why your six months without looking at pornography was not the full forsaking the Lord asks of us, why don't you tell me what the forsaking part of repentance really means?" President Love asked.

"I found a couple of different dictionaries in the bookcase out there. They said things like giving something up, renouncing it, turning away from it entirely, and leaving it forever or giving it up completely. But your article showed me that this is only the beginning. If I have real intent, I won't be satisfied to just shove something out of my life. I will want to replace it with good things that will bring me closer to the Lord and make me more like Him. The obedience that accompanies repentance will help me to love Him more and to value and treasure the commandments and covenants He has blessed me with."

The president leaned back in his chair and smiled. "Elder," he said, "I can't tell you how pleased I am with your growing ability to understand and articulate these principles. That's why we are working together, to learn a better way. I think you are ready to expand obedience to the principle of making restitution. What does that mean to you?"

"Well, I think it means making up for the wrongs you have done. For example, if you stole something, then you would give it back. If you broke something, then you would replace it or at least give fair compensation. If you hurt someone's feelings, you would apologize and try to make it right by being kind and caring."

"Fair enough. That's a good start. Godly sorrow is not just about how bad *we* feel about our sin. It is even more than our yearning desire to stop the sin and replace it with obedience. Genuine remorse would reach outward, past our own feelings, with a sincere concern for how our sin has impacted others. It would motivate us to do whatever it takes and for as long as it takes to make things right and find reconciliation with God and with all those we have offended or injured." He looked through a stack of *Ensign* magazines on his bookshelf, found the one he wanted, located the right page, which was tagged with a Post-it, and handed it to the elder. "Here," he said. "I want you to read this highlighted paragraph from Elder James A. Cullimore of the Seventy."

The elder read, " 'Following confession, the transgressor should demonstrate with good works his repentance, keeping faithfully the commandments of the Lord. Restitution is also an important part of repentance. Restitution, to the degree possible, should be made to restore that which has been taken or to repair the damage that has been done, demonstrating to those offended by his actions his remorse and determination to make amends.' "[1]

The president added, "Elder Curtis, when we have offended or injured or betrayed someone, we should be willing to give that person all the space and all the time they need to regain their trust. This article will explain more about that. Come on back when you're ready."

NOTES

1 "Confession and Forsaking: Elements of Genuine Repentance," *Ensign*, Dec. 1971, 87.

Making Restitution

$\mathcal{E}$lder Curtis sat down calmly. All thoughts of the airport and escape were gone. In fact, he hoped this article might help him envision how he could go about making things right at home, whether from here or—if he had to go—in person. He began to read.

Making Restitution

President Spencer W. Kimball taught: "When a person has experienced the deep sorrow and humility induced by a conviction of sin; when he has cast off the sin and resolutely determined to abhor it henceforth; when he has humbly confessed his sin to God and to the proper persons on earth—when these things are done there remains the requirement of restitution. He must restore that which he damaged, stole or wronged." He further emphasized: "The true spirit of repentance demands that he who injures shall do *everything in his power* to right the wrong" (*The Miracle of Forgiveness*, 191, 195; emphasis added).

He paused to consider what more he could do to right his wrong besides confessing to his bishop and stake president that he had lied. He continued reading.

Making restitution, then, is not as simple or as convenient as paying a traffic ticket, where your debt is measured and specific and all you have to do is pay your fine and you're done with it. The scriptures say that the repentant person must manifest over time that they have "a determination to serve him to the end, and truly manifest by their works that they have received of the Spirit of Christ" (D&C 20:37). President Kimball emphasized this lifelong process when he elaborated: "Repentance means not only to convict yourselves of the horror of the sin, but to confess it, abandon it, and restore to all who have been damaged to the total extent possible; then *spend the balance of your lives* trying to live the commandments of the Lord so he can eventually pardon you and cleanse you" (*The Miracle of Forgiveness*, 200; emphasis added).

In making restitution we are also rebuilding the trust that our sin violated. That usually requires a lengthy period of time. This "willing restitution," observed Elder Richard G. Scott, "is concrete evidence to the Lord that you are committed to do all you can to repent" ("Finding Forgiveness," *Ensign*, May 1995, 76). It also provides such evidence to your family and others that you have injured and with whom you seek to rebuild relationships of trust. President Kimball explained further that the lengthy process of restitution involves more than the mere passing of time. "If a man's actions have brought sorrow and disgrace to his wife and children, in his restitution he must make every effort to restore their confidence and love by an *overabundance of filial devotion and fidelity*. Likewise, if children have wronged their parents, a part of their program of repentance must be to right those wrongs and to honor their parents" (*The Miracle of Forgiveness*, 195; emphasis added). He then gave an example of how one might apply this principle of compensation:

> A man who had confessed infidelity was forgiven by his wife, who saw much in him to commend and believed in his total repentance. To him I said: "Brother Blank, you should from this day forward be the best husband a woman ever had. You should be willing to forgive her little eccentricities, overlook her weaknesses, for she has forgiven you the ten-thousand talent sin and you can afford to forgive numerous little hundred-pence errors" (*The Miracle of Forgiveness*, 195).

Elder Curtis paused to mentally identify those to whom he needed to make restitution. He thought immediately of his bishop and stake president. After all, they were the only ones he had directly lied to. But then he realized that even though his parents had not interviewed him, he had lied to them indirectly by allowing them to assume that he had been found worthy. *So*, he thought, *that's only four people. That won't be so bad.*

The Book of Mormon provides the pattern of lifelong restitution that we are to apply in our repentance. For example, Alma the Younger and the four sons of King Mosiah were involved in a major campaign of "seeking to destroy the church of God" and "to lead astray the people of the Lord, contrary to the commandments of God" (Alma 36:6; Mosiah 27:10). Over time, their work against the Church was highly successful and they became "a great hinderment to the prosperity of the Church of God; stealing away the hearts of the people; causing much dissension among the people; giving a chance for the enemy of God to exercise his power over them" (Mosiah 27:9). Once converted and repentant, however, they did not merely return to obedience and activity in the Church, but they devoted the rest of their lives to making restitution by seeking to become "instruments in the hands of God in bringing many to the knowledge of the truth, yea, to the knowledge of their Redeemer" (Mosiah 27:36).

From the time of their conversion, they traveled together, "round about through all the land, publishing to all the people the things which they had heard and seen, and preaching the word of God in much tribulation, being greatly persecuted by those who were unbelievers, being smitten by many of them. But notwithstanding all this, they did impart much consolation to the Church, confirming their faith, and exhorting them with long-suffering and much travail to keep the commandments of God" (Mosiah 27:32–33). And what was the purpose of this monumental effort? What was the pattern they provided? As "they traveled throughout all the land of Zarahemla, and among all the people who were under the reign of king Mosiah, [they were] *zealously striving to repair all the injuries which they had done to the Church,* confessing all their sins, and publishing all the things which they had seen, and explaining the prophecies and the scriptures to all who desired to hear them" (Mosiah 27:35; emphasis added). Alma served God and His people for the rest of his life. More than twenty years later, he declared, "from that time even until now, *I have labored without ceasing,* that I might bring souls unto repentance; that I might bring them to taste of the exceeding joy of which

I did taste; that they might also be born of God, and be filled with the Holy Ghost" (Alma 36:24; emphasis added). Truly that is the pattern of genuine restitution to which President Kimball and Elder Scott referred.

Feelings of shame drive our thoughts and choices inward so that we selfishly do whatever we can to ease our own discomfort. On the other hand, feelings of godly sorrow and genuine repentance move us to replace concern about ourselves with concern for others, as we see in the examples of Alma and the four sons of Mosiah. The pattern is always the same. For example, as soon as Enos felt successful in his efforts to repent and obtain forgiveness, his heart turned outward, as must ours. "Now, it came to pass that when I had heard these words I began to feel a desire for the welfare of my brethren, the Nephites; wherefore, I did pour out my whole soul unto God for them" (Enos 1:9).

Elder Curtis thought about Alma and the four sons of Mosiah making restitution by serving missions. Could that mean it would be okay for him to stay and serve? He felt encouraged until he realized that they had repented before they were authorized to serve. And he had not yet fully repented. Once again he felt in doubt about his future. He continued to read.

After years of making restitution to the Church among the Nephites, the sons of Mosiah yearned for other opportunities to make restitution because, like Enos, "they were desirous that salvation should be declared to every creature, for they could not bear that any human soul should perish; yea, even the very thoughts that any soul should endure endless torment did cause them to quake and tremble" (Mosiah 28:3). Consequently, they went among their enemies the Lamanites and taught the gospel to them for the next fourteen years (see Alma 17:4). Was that part of their restitution? No—at least not directly. They owed nothing to the Lamanites, for they had not circulated among them, teaching falsehoods, as they had among the Nephites. But it was a way to offer restitution to God that went beyond their specific sins.

Elder Boyd K. Packer taught this expanded principle of restitution when he noted that "the Lord provides ways to pay our debts to Him. In one sense we ourselves may participate in an atonement. When we are willing to restore to others that which we have not taken, or heal wounds that we did not inflict, or pay a debt that we did not incur, we are emulating His part in the Atonement" ("The Brilliant Morning of Forgiveness," *Ensign*, Nov. 1995, 20).

Suddenly, to his dismay, Elder Curtis realized that he had no idea how to make restitution to his parents or priesthood leaders. He had only been thinking in terms of going home and telling them the truth. But that was merely confession. What must he do to make actual restitution? He pondered that question but found no answers. Glumly he returned to the president's office.

Further Discussion on
Making Restitution

*P*resident Love finished his phone call and then greeted the elder. He was not surprised by the look of confusion on his face. "Elder Curtis, is there a problem?" he asked.

"I just realized that I have no idea how to make restitution to my priesthood leaders or my parents. I mean, well, going home and confessing that I lied would be a start, I guess, but I don't see how that makes restitution. I can't go back in time and undo what I did. I lied, and admitting it now, or whenever you send me home, won't change that. I don't see how I can ever make it up to them."

The president said, "I'm glad to see that you've started working on this problem. But let's do it together. It seems to me that before you can plan how to make restitution, you must first identify those whom you have injured by your sin and what the damages were. So let's work on that, and then we can map out a plan of restitution."

Elder Curtis sighed in relief and relaxed in the chair. "Okay," he said, "the first part is easy. The only ones I lied to were the bishop and stake president. But I'm including my parents on the list too. Even though I didn't lie directly to them, the effect was the same because I allowed them to believe that their son was clean and worthy." There, he'd said it. He felt a small measure of satisfaction, as if the journey had begun. But he soon discovered he had only barely cracked open the door.

The president observed, "Let's see, that adds up to four people. Are you sure they are the only ones who were harmed by your deception?"

The elder was about to assure him that yes, that was everyone, but he paused before speaking. *There must be more*, he thought, *or he wouldn't be asking.* But he reluctantly admitted, "That's all I can think of."

"Then let me make some suggestions. This may be discouraging, so I want you to know that the questions I'm going to ask you come from my love and not from condemnation. If you will bear with the pain of honesty, it will lead us to a better place. When you were not truthful with your priesthood leaders, who were they representing?"

He blushed and squirmed in his chair. "I see your point. If you lie to your priesthood leader, it's just like lying to God."

"That's correct. So let's add Him to the list of people to whom you owe restitution. But your list needs to be larger than just the people whom you purposely deceived. For example, let's have you read this scripture."

He took the president's scriptures and read:

> And inasmuch as my people build a house unto me in the name of the Lord, and do not suffer any unclean thing to come into it, that it be not defiled, my glory shall rest upon it;
>
> Yea, and my presence shall be there, for I will come into it, and all the pure in heart that shall come into it shall see God.
>
> But if it be defiled I will not come into it, and my glory shall not be there; for I will not come into unholy temples. (D&C 97:15–17)

"So, Elder, what do you think happened in the temple the day you got your endowment under false pretenses? Did you cause any damage there?"

He slumped in his chair and mumbled, "I guess, because I was unclean and unworthy to be there, I probably ruined it for everyone who came that day. Or at the very least, I must have diminished the Spirit there. But how could I ever undo that?"

"We'll worry about the restitution part later. For now, I want you to consider how your deception has also injured your investigators."

Elder Curtis's face paled. "I guess I cheated them by being less spiritual than I could have been—less than I should have been. By being a dishonest representative of the Lord, I denied them the spiritual influence they might have received if I had been worthy to be more fully in tune with the Holy Ghost."

"Being less than we should be is a problem we all face, but speaking of diminished influence, have you and your companion ever been asked to administer to someone who was ill?"

"Yes, we have, several times."

"And were you able to do that with the faith and confidence that you could discern and speak the will of the Lord, or did you just go through the motions?"

"I felt empty and without faith. I always tried to do the anointing so that my companion would be the voice for the blessing."

"And what about your companions? What is the damage to them?"

"It's the same," he admitted dejectedly. "Companions are supposed to teach and uplift and help each other. I never could do that. Not just because I was unworthy but also because subconsciously, I was always stewing about my secret."

"Which brings us to the next victim."

"I can't think who that would be."

"What about you, yourself?" the president asked kindly. "I think that all of the harm that you inflicted on God's temple, your investigators, and your companions, you also inflicted upon yourself. In fact," he asked tenderly, "isn't it true that you have suffered more from your sin than anyone else?"

The elder replied hesitantly, "Yes, I guess that's true, but I hadn't realized it until now."

"It's a scriptural principle, Elder. Here, read this."

The elder read, " 'Now I would that ye should see that they brought upon themselves the curse; and even so doth every man that is cursed bring upon himself his own condemnation' (Alma 3:19)."

Elder Curtis gulped. He said, "It never stops, does it!"

The president smiled but said nothing.

"How can you smile at all this?" the elder asked. "I feel terrible."

"You're right; it is terrible. But I'm smiling because I think we are making progress." President Love remained silent for a couple of minutes. He prayed silently for the elder who was pondering the expanding debt of repentance and restitution that he owed.

When the elder finally spoke, his voice shook and he sounded discouraged. "There's no way out of this," he groaned. "Even when I go home and confess to those I've wronged, it won't undo what I did. I can't fix the temple. I can't fix the investigators or companions I've cheated. I can't give myself back the experiences I've missed. Like the article explained, making restitution is not as simple as paying a fine. There's no way to undo all of this. How can I ever make restitution for what I've done?" he asked, on the verge of tears.

"Perhaps you can't," said the president, "but there is still hope." He reached for President Kimball's book on the shelf, browsed a moment, and then said, "Here, read what President Kimball taught about your situation."

The elder took the book and read, " 'The repentant sinner is required to make restitution insofar as it is possible. I say "insofar as it is possible" because there are some sins for which no adequate restitution can be made, and others for which only partial restitution is possible.' "[1]

"That's what I mean," lamented the elder in great distress. "If I can't make restitution, then how can I repent? If I can't put things back together the way they were supposed to be, how can I ever feel right about myself or the damage I've done?"

"Elder, you already know the answer to that. Whenever there are things that we cannot personally make right, then we must turn them over to the grace of the Lord, who, through the Atonement, has infinite power to compensate for every human deficiency." He opened his resource drawer and found an article by Elder Packer. Handing it to the elder, he said, "Here's something I want you to have. You can study it later, but for now, read this part that I have highlighted and then we'll talk about the specifics of what you can do to make restitution." The elder read:

> To earn forgiveness, one must make restitution. *That means you give back what you have taken or ease the pain of those you have injured. But sometimes you cannot give back what you have taken because you don't have it to give.* If you have caused others to suffer unbearably—defiled someone's virtue, for example—it is not within your power to give it back. *There are times you cannot mend that which you have broken.* Perhaps the offense was long ago, or the injured refused your penance. *Perhaps the damage was so severe that you cannot fix it no matter how desperately you want to.*

Your repentance cannot be accepted unless there is a restitution. *If you cannot undo what you have done, you are trapped.* It is easy to understand how helpless and hopeless you then feel and why you might want to give up, just as Alma did. The thought that rescued Alma, when he acted upon it, is this: Restoring what you cannot restore, healing the wound you cannot heal, fixing that which you broke and you cannot fix is the very purpose of the Atonement of Christ.

When your desire is firm and you are willing to pay the "uttermost farthing" (see Matthew 5:25–26), *the law of restitution is suspended. Your obligation is transferred to the Lord. He will settle your accounts.* [2]

"So you see, Elder, it is not as hopeless as you thought. The good news and glad tidings of the gospel are that Jesus Christ can take away the guilt and punishment and even some of the consequences of our mistakes. Elder D. Todd Christofferson of the Seventy taught: 'The power of His Atonement *can erase the effects of sin in us.* When we repent, His atoning grace justifies and cleanses us (see 3 Nephi 27:16–20). *It is as if we had not succumbed, as if we had not yielded to temptation.*' "[3]

"Elder, when we willingly and sincerely do all that we can do, we may be sure of Him doing the rest. So let's look at what you can and can't do. For example, you obviously need to confess your deception to your parents and priesthood leaders. That won't undo the lie, but you could make sure that from now on you are totally honest—not only in temple recommend interviews but also in your prayers and relationships. Can you see that as a form of restitution?"

"Yes, I can."

"Here's another example. There is no way that you can go back in time and undefile the temple. But can you make sure that from now on you are clean and pure when you enter a temple? Can you make sure that from now on whenever you go into a temple, your presence will add to the Spirit inside rather than detract from it? Can you make sure that you reverence the temple as God's house and never take the privilege of attending for granted? Can you see how doing things like this could be accepted by the Lord as an effort to make restitution to His holy house?"

"Yes."

"Can you see any way to go back in time and reverse the lack of spiritual influence that your unworthiness robbed from your investigators or companions?"

"No, I can't. There is no way to even measure it, much less to undo it."

"That's right. But couldn't you make sure that from now on you will never give another missionary discussion, another talk, or teach another class without preparing and seeking the help of the Spirit? Couldn't you make sure that from now on you work on every relationship with love and caring and concern? Couldn't you become the kind of person that always tries to lift others, to nourish and cheer and encourage them? Can you see how doing things like these would show God your desire to make restitution?"

"Yes," he exclaimed, growing excited and hopeful.

"I'd like to quote to you one of my favorite encouragement scriptures. It says: 'Therefore, dearly beloved brethren, let us cheerfully do all things that lie in our power; and then may we stand still, with the utmost assurance, to see the salvation of God, and for his arm to be revealed.' That's in D&C 123:17.

"All these things I've been suggesting to you for restitution really amount to keeping your covenants, being true and faithful, and trying to become like Christ. That's what we are all supposed to be working on anyway. If you will dedicate the rest of your life to becoming an instrument in His work as a valiant disciple of Christ, then you will make it possible for Him to accept your repentance. Those are the glad tidings of the gospel. You need the faith to accept it for yourself and the faith to share it with others. If you will do that, then I know He will give you peace and forgiveness and compensate for whatever damages you cannot personally undo."

Elder Curtis was actually smiling with excitement. His eyes glowed with peace and he waited for the president to finish.

"I want you to realize that no one is perfect; we all slip back once in awhile. You will need to understand this and have compassion as you work with other people. Sometimes people waver in their repentance process because their resolve falters. Sometimes it is just because we are fallen beings and subject to human weakness." As he handed him another article to study, he said, "Elder Curtis, this will help you to understand that our imperfections are not as dangerous as are the self-defeating attitudes that we often adopt about our inability to be as good as we intend to be."

As the elder returned to his cubicle, the president went to coordinate things with Sister Richardson and let her know that he could probably return to his normal schedule by the next day. With zone conferences just a few days away, he knew she would be glad of that. So was he. Based on his interviews with Elder Curtis and other missionaries, he now had the agenda for his zone conference talks.

NOTES

1 *The Miracle of Forgiveness*, 194.

2 Boyd K. Packer, "The Brilliant Morning of Forgiveness," *Ensign*, Nov. 1995, 19–20; emphasis added.

3 "That They May Be One in Us," *Ensign*, Nov. 2002, 71; emphasis added.

Relapse

$\mathcal{E}$lder Curtis returned to his cubicle, eager to read about this new subject and expecting it to provide some real encouragement. But before beginning, he knelt in prayer. He didn't notice how each prayer he offered was moving steadily away from confusion and pleading and toward focusing on his gratitude and worship. Had he noticed, he would have realized what a healthy indicator that was of his improving spirituality. He settled into his chair and began to read.

Relapse

A person may decide to repent in a flash of time—an instant resolution. But the reality of our mortal condition is that it will take much more time to implement and sustain that choice in the face of life's continuing temptations. It is always easier to *mean* well than it is to *do* well. To conquer the fallen flesh requires a lifetime of persistent effort and determination. It is not reasonable to expect virtue, holiness, and victory over our fallen natures to be manifest from one single choice or event.

It is understandable that when we finally make a real commitment to repent and improve our lives, we are anxious to get on with it and have it done. We don't want to deal with discouraging relapses. But the process of learning and improving often involves stumbling through bad choices, learning from our mistakes, and repenting over and over as we renew our resolves and efforts. When the Lord counseled: "Ye must practise virtue and holiness before me *continually*" (D&C 46:33; emphasis added), He was talking about the enduring-to-the-end process and showing us that He never expected us to get things right with one or two attempts.

Elder Neal A. Maxwell taught, "The scriptural advice, 'Do not run faster or labor more than you have strength' (D&C 10:4) suggests paced progress, much as God used seven creative periods in preparing man and this earth. There is a difference, therefore, between being 'anxiously engaged' and being over-anxious and thus underengaged" ("Notwithstanding My Weakness," *Ensign*, Nov. 1976, 12–13).

Over-anxious and underengaged, mused the elder. *No wonder I've been so ineffective in my work. But aren't we supposed to be anxious about repenting of our faults? How does one generate the urgency needed to make changes without becoming so concerned about it that we defeat ourselves with too much anxiety?*

Elder Merrill J. Bateman cautioned, "For most of us, this spiritual rebirth process stretches across a lifetime and into the next, as we are refined one step and one principle at a time" ("Becoming a Disciple of Christ," *Ensign*, Apr. 2006, 22). Elder Bruce C. Hafen taught concerning these same vital issues:

> But growth means growing pains. It also means learning from our mistakes in a continual process made possible by the Savior's grace, which He extends both during and "after all we can do" (2 Nephi 25:23). . . .
>
> His plan is developmental—line upon line, step by step, grace for grace. So if you have problems in your life, don't assume there is something wrong with you. Struggling with those problems is at the very core of life's purpose. As we draw close to God, He will show us our weaknesses and through them make us wiser, stronger (see Ether 12:27). If you're seeing more of your weaknesses, that just might mean you're moving nearer to God, not farther away. ("The Atonement: All for All," *Ensign*, May 2004, 97)

Expecting too much of ourselves too soon, without patience for the enduring-to-the-end process, sets us up for disappointment when we find that we cannot perfect ourselves as quickly as we had hoped to.

Elder Curtis paused to enjoy that encouragement. *Wow*, he thought, *all of this pain I've been going through does not mean I'm getting worse but that I'm ready to get better!*

Another reason for unnecessary discouragement in the repentance process is the incorrect assumption that being "born again" or receiving "the mighty change" of heart and nature means that instantly and forever, our battles are over. We incorrectly assume that we no longer have to face resisting temptations or overcoming mortal weaknesses and sins. But why would the Savior command: "Let the church take heed and pray always, lest they fall into temptation" (D&C 20:33) if He did not expect us to be vulnerable to temptations throughout our entire mortality?

Many people envision sincere repentance as an uninterrupted path leading up an incline. However, more realistically, it will be a series of ups and downs, as we mean to do right, but slip occasionally and then renew our efforts. Each cycle of learning to distinguish between good and evil makes us a little wiser. Someday, in a better place and time, we will "rest" from those struggles, but for now, in this mortal testing ground, that is an unreasonable expectation.

Therapist Rod W. Jeppson gave this encouraging counsel: "When you falter, take a few moments alone and ponder how far you have come in your healing process. Satan wants you to believe the lie that a lapse is evidence that you have made no progress and that you will never be able to change. This simply is not true. After a lapse, give yourself credit for all the little things you have done right that have put you on the pathway to healing" ("Relapse Prevention," in *Confronting Pornography*, 273–74).

President Gordon B. Hinckley's words validate that advice. He stated: "Those changes may not be measurable in a day or a week or a month. Resolutions are quickly made and quickly forgotten. But, in a year from now, if we are doing better than we have done in the past, then the efforts of these days will not have been in vain" ("An Humble and a Contrite Heart," *Ensign*, Nov. 2000, 88).

BYU professor Robert L. Millet provided similar encouragement when he wrote: "Character is not a product of a sinless life, not a result of never making a mistake or an error of judgment, but rather of never staying down when we have fallen. We show what we're made of and of our determination to follow the Christ by getting up and dusting ourselves off one more time than we fall" (*Are We There Yet?*, 116).

These two tree stumps symbolize the persistence and determination that we need to pick ourselves up and continue onward, always just one more time than we stumble and fall. Their life was supposedly aborted, but they refused to give up and are coming back, just like we can, even in the face of total disappointment and failure.

"That is what you are doing, Elder," the Spirit whispered. "You are picking yourself up in an attempt to get this right, and the Lord is pleased with your efforts." He was not used to such communications and looked around the office, startled, not certain if someone had spoken to him or if the thoughts had just appeared in his mind. Seeing no one nearby, he made a mental note to ask the president about it and then continued reading.

All of our efforts to repent and change behavior are but preliminary and preparatory to receiving the mighty change that will come as Christ blesses us with the "born again" process. One reason that we have unrealistic expectations is that we misinterpret the scriptural examples of conversion of people like Paul, Alma, and Enos. But those accounts are condensed. They don't explicitly tell of the continued struggles that occurred after the initial events of their conversion. Elder Merrill J. Bateman reminded us of the lifelong process when he emphasized: "Few mortals share with Alma the Younger or Paul the Apostle the dramatic experiences which resulted in their spiritual rebirths over short periods of time. In fact, I believe those experiences are recorded in the scriptures *not to define the time frame* during which one may be reborn but to provide a vivid picture of what the *accumulated*, subtle changes are that take place in a faithful person *over a lifetime*" ("Living a Christ-Centered Life," *Ensign*, Jan. 1999, 7; emphasis added).

It is human nature to want that to happen sooner, rather than later, so it is important to remember that the Lord is in charge. And in something as important as transforming our fallen natures, He will not be rushed. When we give our life to Him, He will be rebuilding us for eternity. While we may wish for results faster than they come, He may have a purpose for going slower if, in His wisdom, that will produce a stronger and more stable character.

As the God of all power, He could most certainly heal us instantly. So if He sees fit to take longer in changing us than we wish for, we must learn not to stamp our feet and demand instant perfection and recovery. We know that He will grant the changes and transformations we need as quickly as we are prepared to receive them, because He has promised: "I will order all things for your good, as fast as ye are able to receive them" (D&C 111:11). Not only must we learn to trust His timing, but we also must be grateful that He cares enough to allow as much time as He feels we need to finally get it right.

The elder hurried into the office, pleased that the president was not on the phone this time.

Further Discussion on
Relapse

"You look pleased, Elder Curtis. What are your thoughts?"

"Well, I learned a lot, just like with every article you give me. But I guess the best thing was something that happened to me as I studied. I think it was an inspiration from the Spirit."

The president replied, "Well that would certainly be a good sign. Before you tell me what it was, let's review a scripture that will help you to decide if you just thought of it yourself or if it was a message sent to you by your Heavenly Father. Read in Moroni chapter seven, verse thirteen."

The elder opened his Book of Mormon and read: " 'But behold, that which is of God inviteth and enticeth to do good continually; wherefore, every thing which inviteth and enticeth to do good, and to love God, and to serve him, is inspired of God.' "

"Thank you. So what do you think? Did your thoughts edify and entice you to come closer to God?"

"Yes, they did. It was as if the Spirit was telling me that I had done the right thing by coming to you." Suddenly he felt a little embarrassed. "I guess I should have already known that."

"Elder Curtis, not every message from the Spirit is to reveal new things to us. Many times it is just a way for the Lord to put His arm around us and confirm something we already know or to assure us of His love. I'm not at all surprised that you had that experience. You need to remember how you felt when the message came because it will help to sustain you through the difficult times yet to come, as you begin to apply what we've been learning.

"So, let's review the relapse principles together. Many times, the more sincerely someone is trying to repent, the more they will beat on themselves for their temporary failures. It is common for them to mistakenly think that the more times they slip on their resolves and repeat their sins or weaknesses, the worse a person they are. And, if they are deliberately sinning—carelessly, thoughtlessly, and deliberately—then perhaps they should feel that way. But if someone's unintended relapses are merely the result of human weakness, then that is not the same thing as deliberate hypocrisy or mocking God. In fact, I believe that the longer a person has struggled to overcome a particular sin, the fact that they are still trying does not reflect how weak they are but rather the strength and integrity of their character."

"President," said the elder excitedly, "that's kind of what the Spirit said to me." He paused to reflect a moment, and then he said, "But aren't we supposed to feel bad when we think about our sins? I mean, well, I think the Spirit said the Lord was pleased that I came to you, but that doesn't erase what I did. Shouldn't I still feel bad about that?"

"Of course people should feel bad when they sin, even if it is an unintentional relapse. But they should regard such feelings as a blessing, for they indicate the presence of a healthy conscience and godly sorrow. In contrast, not feeling pain for a relapse would be a terrible sign of indifference. You see, you weren't indifferent all those months that you hid your sin. You were just scared and stubborn." He chuckled, to the surprise of the elder.

"However," President Love continued, "the appropriate response to an unintended relapse should not be something like the self-condemning 'bad dog' or 'shame-on-me' attacks that we talked about yesterday. More productive would be a balance between patience with our humanness and enough godly discontent that we refuse to settle for it."

As the president opened his resource drawer and removed another article, he said, "Thank you for pondering how to balance these things out. That is the purpose of your next article, so take this back to your work area and see if this doesn't help. Come on back when you're ready."

To Live with Regret or Hope

Elder Curtis noticed the time with concern. He'd already had lunch with the president's family, and the afternoon was melting away. He felt he'd come so far, but he wanted to make sure they had time to do all that the president had in mind because he expected that he would probably have to rejoin his companion that evening. He felt an urgency to continue his study but paused first to pray for understanding before picking up the article.

To Live with Regret or Hope

No amount of regret will permit us to relive the past, nor can we live in tomorrow. In reality, we cannot even live in today, for most of that lies in our future as well. We have only the present moment. Moses was trying to help a people who knew God only in the past—or in their hopes for the future. For centuries they had treasured the knowledge that Jehovah had been real to Abraham, Isaac, and Jacob. In their minds this isolated Him as a God of the past—the God of "I Was." And they dreamed of some future day when Jehovah would once again act on their behalf, in fulfillment of His past promises to the three patriarchs. To them, it also isolated Him as the distant God of "I Will Be." The Lord sent Moses to teach

Israel (and us) to know our Savior as the God of "I Am," the God of the present, the God of right now.

Elder Jeffrey R. Holland stated: "God has declared himself in the present tense. I am the Great I Am." He further emphasized:

> In addition to, and more important than, Jesus' past and future life is his eternal presence. That is, Christ is not only Alpha and Omega, he is Alpha *through* Omega—complete, abiding, permanent, unchanged. As well as being before and after us, Christ will, if we choose, be with us. The great challenge of our lives is usually not meditating on what we once were or wishing on what we may yet become, but rather *living in the present moment as God would have us live.* Fortunately, Christ can be in that moment for each of us since "all things are present" before him (D&C 38:2) and "time only is measured unto men" (Alma 40:8). ("Whom Say Ye That I Am?" *Ensign*, Sept. 1974, 7; emphasis added)

Elder Curtis thought, *Wow! That's exactly what I've done all my life. I've only thought of Christ as being back in the New Testament or Book of Mormon, or sometime in the future, in the Second Coming. I realize now that I've never pictured Him right here in my own time as a living Savior.* He could sense how that perspective would change a person's relationship with God. In fact, it should change everything.

Kenneth L. Higbee, a BYU Professor of Psychology, pointed out:

> Too many people make themselves miserable by dwelling needlessly on their past failures and mistakes. They lie awake at night agonizing over the mistakes they have made and what they should have done. Almost everyone occasionally does thoughtless, impulsive things that bring unpleasant consequences. Almost everyone occasionally misses golden opportunities through apathy or oversight. Almost everyone may be occasionally selfish or unkind. We cannot help feeling despair over such occasions, but we should not feel as if we ought to be exiled from the human race simply because of them." ("Forgetting Those Things Which Are Behind," *Ensign*, Sept. 1972, 83)

Focusing too much on the mistakes of the past can result in great spiritual harm. If we are constantly condemning ourselves for past mistakes and sins, this abuse of our mind makes us our own worst enemy. With that negative focus, by the very act of dwelling on, analyzing, regretting, pondering, and forcing our minds to revolve around a problem in the past, we can actually increase its strength and unwittingly perpetuate the very thing we were trying to overcome.

Our preoccupation with the past is like setting up a mental video that never stops. Over and over it replays painful memories. This causes the person to sink lower and lower into despair and self-loathing. As Elder Neal A. Maxwell explained, "Some of us who would not chastise a neighbor for his frailties have a field day with our own. . . . We should, of course, learn from our mistakes, but *without forever studying the instant replays* as if these were the game of life itself" ("Not Withstanding My Weakness, *Ensign*, Nov. 1976, 13–14; emphasis added). And so, concluded Elder Jeffrey R. Holland, "The past is to be learned from, not lived in, and the future is to be planned for, not for us to be paralyzed by" ("Whom Say Ye That I Am?," *Ensign*, Sept. 1974, 7).

BYU Professor Truman G. Madsen described Satan's effort to overemphasize past mistakes as one of his strategies or tricks.

> If there are some of you who have been tricked into the conviction that you have gone too far, that you have been weighed down with doubts on which you alone have a monopoly, that you have had the poison of sin which makes it impossible ever again to be what you could have been—then hear me. I bear testimony that you cannot sink farther than the light and sweeping intelligence of Jesus Christ can reach. I bear testimony that as long as there is one spark of the will to repent and to reach, he is there. He did not just descend to your condition; he descended below it, "that he might be in all and through all things, the light of truth" (D&C 88:6). (*Christ and the Inner Life*, 14)

Satan knows that a heart hurting from despair and hopelessness affects every part of our life. As we become more negative and pessimistic, our mental and emotional energy drains away, and we feel empty and hollow, stripped of the will to fight back. Without hope, we lose confidence in God. We may even doubt His power and willingness to deliver us. If so, the powers of evil rejoice because they know that once we give up and separate ourselves from God, our spiritual progress is stopped.

The scriptures provide clear counsel on how to combat these attacks. For example, Paul certainly had many things in his past to mourn and regret when he had been an active enemy to Christ and His Church. But he knew it was important to let go of his past mistakes and focus on the goals of the future. He said, "But this one thing I do, *forgetting those things which are behind*, and reaching forth unto those things which are before, *I press toward the mark* for the prize of the high calling of God in Christ Jesus" (Philippians 3:13–14; emphasis added). We must do the same. As Nephi counseled, "*Ye must press forward* with a steadfastness in Christ, having a perfect brightness of hope, and a love of God and of all men." And then he added this encouraging promise: "Wherefore, if ye shall press forward, feasting upon the word of Christ, and endure to the end, behold, thus saith the Father: *Ye shall have eternal life*" (2 Nephi 31:20; emphasis added).

We cannot continue to live in despair when we understand Christ's love—that He came into this world to rescue us from our sins and that He will assist and reward our repentance because every person is of inestimable worth to Him. As we remember that no matter what lies in our past, our future is spotless, we will be encouraged to let go of the past and reach for the future with joyful expectation.

That's exactly what Elder Curtis was looking forward to. He hurried back to the president's office.

Further Discussion on
Hope

elcome back, Elder. What do you feel is the most important thing you learned from this article?"

"Without a doubt, it's that once I repent and make things right with the Lord, I not only have the right but also the duty to let go of the past and press forward in becoming a better disciple."

The president smiled in satisfaction. "Wonderful!" he said. "Are there any questions?"

"Yes, there are. I do understand what you've taught me about the past and the future. But I have this gnawing doubt about when it is okay to forget the past. It almost sounds like dismissing reality and clinging to positive thinking to get out of our deserved punishments. I know that can't be what is meant."

President Love replied, "It's always good to think positively instead of negatively. But our expectations must be based on gospel truths and not on empty platitudes. The scriptures teach that we cannot be saved without hope. No matter what lies in our past, we only lose hope when we lose our grasp on the 'glad tidings' of the gospel. Unlike the Savior, who dismisses our forgiven sins from His memory, we can still remember them when we look back. But those memories should not torment us as they did before we repented. Of course, our godly sorrow temporarily reminds us of the past. That is its job. But once we resolve those mistakes, that same godly sorrow should draw us forward and upward, toward the Savior. As Elder Marvin J. Ashton commented, "Where you've been is not nearly as important as where you are and where you're going."[1] Hearing that from an apostle should strengthen your hope.

"As for not deserving to escape the punishment, let's put it this way. Every choice and every action has consequences. The consequences that are linked to our disobedience are not there because God is vindictive and wants to get even by making us pay. It is because of His love and desire to help us learn (see Alma 42). When we have learned to be obedient, the chastening has served its purpose, so we let it go and move on.

"Let's read what Elder Jeffrey R. Holland taught about how we move past satanic taunts over our past mistakes." He sorted through a stack of Church magazines, found the one he wanted, opened to a Post-it tag, and handed it to the elder. "Read the part I've highlighted," he said.

The elder read:

> Here your most crucial challenge, once recognizing the seriousness of your mistakes, will be to believe that you can change, that there can be a different you. To disbelieve that is clearly a Satanic device designed to discourage and defeat you. . . . Only he would say, "You can't change. You won't change. It's too long and too hard to change. Give up. Give in. Don't repent. You are just the way you are." That, my friends, is a lie born of desperation. Don't fall for it.[2]

Elder Curtis didn't want to anger the president, so he said carefully, "Still, even when we let go of the past and try to do better, we continue to make mistakes, and then the memory of all those previous mistakes comes pouring back in."

President Love replied, "Elder, that's the whole point of this discussion. Do you think Paul was able to forget all the terrible things in his past with just one resolve, or that he might have had to let go of those things many times throughout his life? Progression is just that: progression, one step at a time. And sometimes we have to repeat the same steps many times. Just remember that as long as we are moving forward, no matter how slowly or stumblingly, we have a right and a duty to cling to our hope in Christ.

"A long time ago I decided to memorize something that President Ezra Taft Benson taught, and I'm so glad I did because it has carried me through many of my own times of doubt. He counseled: 'We must not lose hope. Hope is an anchor to the souls of men. Satan would have us cast away that anchor. In this way he can bring discouragement and surrender. But we must not lose hope.'³

"You'll find this all makes more sense to you after you've had another chance to read and ponder and pray about each article I've given you. Now, Elder, we only have one more subject to discuss, so I've arranged for Elder Jones to come by and pick you up in a couple of hours."

"I'd be thrilled to go back to work, but how can I do that when we haven't even discussed whether I have to go home or not?"

"I'm going to give you a couple of days to ponder that, and then we'll talk again in your interview after the zone conference. Before we continue, I want you to go take a walk in the backyard while I make some calls. I see you have a watch, so you go out and clear your head and then come back in about fifteen minutes."

***

When Elder Curtis returned, the president said, "Elder Curtis, we are now coming to the end of our studies together. The doctrine of confession is one that would normally occur at the beginning of the repentance process. But I have saved it for last because this will be the launch pad for whatever action you decide to take and I want you to have a doctrinal foundation for your decision.

"I'm sure you know that when someone is tried for a crime in a regular court of justice, the usual legal advice from their defense attorney is to deny everything and admit nothing, placing the full burden of proof on the prosecutors. God, however, is not a prosecutor. He is our Father, and He is on our side. Rather than to convict and punish, God's goal is to rescue and heal. So when we break God's commandments, the best practice is full confession, which leads to full repentance, forgiveness, healing, and the transfer of our debt to the Atonement of Jesus Christ."

President Love noticed that Elder Curtis was squirming in his chair. He said, "Elder Curtis, I want you to learn that confession is not a punishment but an opportunity. But I can understand why even people who sincerely want to change their lives and improve their obedience often dread it. I want to share some ideas with you that might put confession in a new light. You go on back to your work area for your last study session, and when you are ready for our final talk today, come on back."

NOTES

1 In Sheri L. Dew, "As Elder Statesman," *This People*, Mar./Apr. 1984, 27.

2 "For Times of Trouble," *New Era*, Oct. 1980, 11–12.

3 "A Mighty Change of Heart," *Ensign*, Oct. 1989, 5.

The Opportunity of Confession

As Elder Curtis sat down to study the article, he knew exactly what the president had meant about this subject being a launching pad, or starting point, for the direction of his repentance. Nothing would ever be right until he did what he could to correct his lies to his family and priesthood leaders. Would he have to go home to do that? Could it be done by phone or by mail? Why hadn't the president spelled this out for him? He began to read.

The Opportunity of Confession

Heavenly Father is a God of light and truth, while Satan is the master of darkness, lies, deception, and secrets. When we avoid confession, we move away from God and toward Satan. When we confess, as commanded, we move toward light and healing—we move toward God.

He thought, *This is so obvious. Why didn't I realize that back home when I covered things up? This is what I want to do now. I don't care what it takes. I want to make things right. I want to be right.* The article continued:

So inescapable are the consequences of these two choices that

President Kimball stated that proper confession "indicates the sinner's conviction of sin and his desire to abandon the evil practices." In fact, he even described it as *"one of the tests* of true repentance, for, 'By this ye may know if a man repenteth of his sins—behold, he will confess them and forsake them' (D&C 58:43)" (*The Miracle of Forgiveness*, 181, 177; emphasis added). Elder J. Richard Clarke, then a counselor in the Presiding Bishopric, also regarded confession as part of the test. He explained, "Confession is a necessary requirement for complete forgiveness. It is an indication of true 'godly sorrow.' It is part of the cleansing process. Starting anew requires a clean page in the diary of our conscience" ("Confession," *New Era*, Nov. 1980, 4). Christian author Don Baker also helps us understand the essentiality of this commandment. He emphasized:

> It is confession that *starts* the process of forgiving. It is a healthy, healing thing to drop all evasions and say that you have failed, sinned, blundered, hurt someone, disappointed yourself. This is the place to start. Admit it. All else comes later. *Until you get over this hurdle, you have not started the race.* Until you open this door, the fresh air and sunshine that awaits you will be locked out. (*Forgiving Yourself,* 23)

The Benefits of Proper Confession

We cannot complete a successful repentance as long as we hide our sins and fail to confess them. The Lord has promised many blessings to those who obey this commandment. One blessing is the return of help from the Holy Ghost. As Elder Neal A. Maxwell explained, "True repentance also includes confession: 'Now therefore make confession unto the Lord God of your fathers' (Ezra 10:11). One with a broken heart will not hold back. As confession lets the sickening sin empty out, then the Spirit which withdrew returns to renew" ("Repentance," *Ensign*, Nov. 1991, 31).

Another blessing is the forgiveness that transfers our debt to the Savior. "The Lord suffered and died so that your sins could be paid for by him, rather than by you. But it can only work if you do your part—by confessing and forsaking your sin. And the sooner this is done, the sooner the sweetness and joy of that forgiveness can surround you" ("Questions and Answers," *New Era*, Oct. 1989, 18). This principle was verified by Christ when He said, "I, the Lord, forgive sins unto those who confess their sins before me and ask forgiveness, who have not sinned unto death" (D&C 64:7). We cannot expect His Atonement to apply to our sins if we shortcut the divinely prescribed procedure by failing to confess them as part of our repentance.

Yet another major benefit of proper confession is a lessening of the burden of sin. We can see this principle verified in the words of our prophets, professional counselors, and therapists and from sinners who have shared their experiences. For example, President Kimball explained: "Confession is not only the revealing of errors to proper authorities, but the sharing of burdens to lighten them. One lifts at least part of his burden and places it on other shoulders which are able and willing to help carry the load. Then there comes satisfaction in having taken another step in doing all that is possible to rid oneself of the burden of transgression" (*The Miracle of Forgiveness*, 187–88).

Director of Family Life at BYU, Professor James M. Harper wrote: "The act of confession lifts mental and emotional weight off the spiritual shoulders. Once we can move past the embarrassment we fear to do this to the proper people, our energy can then direct to change and improvement. But until we 'come clean' with our leaders, families and most importantly, the Lord, we are stuck in a quagmire" (in "The Role of Shame in Pornography Problems," *Confronting Pornography*, 121). These principles are illustrated in the following statement:

> As I began my confession, I felt a very heavy burden lifting from me. Instead of the confession *increasing* my pain, each confessed sin seemed to *reduce* the weight of my burden. When I was done they asked if there was anything else that I should mention. What a great relief it was to be able to say "No, that was everything." I felt as though an enormous weight had been lifted from my shoulders. (Gerald and LoAnne Curtis, *The Worth of Every Soul*, 54)

Elder Curtis paused to lament that he had not had the courage to deserve these blessings as he prepared for his mission. But the pause was brief because he now had a testimony that peace would come to him soon, when he did make those confessions to the folks back home.

To Whom Must We Make Confession?

PRIVATE CONFESSION: We should confess our sins to ourselves as well as to Heavenly Father. As President Spencer W. Kimball explained, "The next step, confession of the sin, is a very important aspect of repentance. We must confess and admit our sins to ourselves and then seriously begin the process of repentance. We must also confess our sins to our Heavenly Father" ("The Gospel of Repentance," *Ensign*, Oct. 1982, 4). Beyond that, we owe confession wherever possible and appropriate, to each and every person that we have betrayed, hurt, or offended by our misconduct. "You always need to confess your sins to the Lord. You should also confess your sins to those you have wronged. If you have committed serious sins, such as immorality, you need to confess them to your bishop" (*For the Strength of Youth*, 30).

CONFESSION TO OTHERS: President Harold B. Lee taught us when to confess to others. He said, "That confession must be made first to him or her who has been most wronged by your acts" (*Youth and the Church*, 99). President Spencer W. Kimball also described this form of confession to friends and family members when he explained, "While the major sins . . . call for confession to the proper Church authorities, clearly such confession is neither necessary nor desirable for all sins. Those of lesser gravity but which have offended others—marital differences, minor fits of anger, disagreements and such—should instead be confessed to the person or persons hurt and the matter should be cleared between the persons involved, normally without a reference to a Church authority" (*The Miracle of Forgiveness*, 185).

PUBLIC CONFESSION: Most of the time our sins are of a private nature, which means that our confessions should also be private rather than public. However, as President Harold B. Lee explained, "If you have 'offended many persons openly,' your acknowledgment is to be made openly and before those whom you have offended that you might show your shame and humility and willingness to receive a merited rebuke" (*Youth and the Church*, 99).

We see a pattern for public confession in the life of Corianton, whose immoral conduct on his mission to the Zoramites became so widely known that it hurt the reputation of the Church and the other missionaries. As his father, Alma, the prophet and president of the Church, taught him how to repent, he first pointed out the damage he had done: "Behold, O my son, how great iniquity ye brought upon the Zoramites; for when they saw your conduct they would not believe in my words" (Alma 39:11). Then he challenged him to repent, saying, "And now the Spirit of the Lord doth say unto me: Command thy children to do good, lest they lead away the hearts of many people to destruction; therefore I command you, my son, in the fear of God, that ye refrain from your iniquities" (Alma 39:12). Finally, he set the pattern for public confession when he required Corianton to go back to the very Zoramites he had betrayed and confess his immorality: "That ye turn to the Lord with all your mind, might, and strength; that ye lead away the hearts of no more [people] to do wickedly; but rather *return unto them, and acknowledge your faults* and that wrong which ye have done" (Alma 39:13; emphasis added). Alma and the four sons of Mosiah, who had gone about publicly trying to destroy the Church, also went back to the very same people to confess their errors and try to undo the lies with which they had misled them.

> And they traveled throughout all the land of Zarahemla, and among all the people who were under the reign of king Mosiah, zealously striving to repair all the injuries which they had done to the church, *confessing all their sins*, and publishing all the things which they had seen, and explaining the prophecies and the scriptures to all who desired to hear them. (Mosiah 27:35; emphasis added)

CONFESSION TO PRIESTHOOD LEADERS: President Kimball recognized that "confession is one of the hardest of all obstacles for the repenting sinner to negotiate." He lamented, "His shame often restrains him from making known his guilt and acknowledging his error. Sometimes his assumed lack of confidence in mortals to whom he should confess his sin justifies in his mind his keeping the secret locked in his own heart" (*The Miracle of Forgiveness*, 178). President Kimball also encouraged us to remember that "every member of the Church is given a bishop or branch president who through his very priesthood ordination or calling is a 'judge in Israel.' In these matters," he comforted, "the bishop is our best earthly friend. He is one who works with the Spirit of the Lord in blessing our lives and he keeps all matters completely confidential" ("The Gospel of Repentance," *Ensign*, Oct. 1982, 2). Hiding our problems from our priesthood leaders harms our spirituality and delays our healing. "The truth is that your bishop has been called of God because he is a compassionate and godly man who wants to help. He is God's agent on earth to hear your confession. He can help you get on the road to repentance and forgiveness and the unspeakable joy which comes from knowing your sins have been forgiven" ("Questions and Answers," *New Era*, Oct. 1989, 17).

Elder Curtis paused again, filled with a new and unfamiliar remorse. He was used to the guilt that he felt for lying to his priesthood leaders. But he was now discovering a new pain. It was the realization of how little he had thought of his bishop and stake president. As he pondered these feelings he realized that it was not just them that he had failed to respect and trust. It was also the Lord who had chosen them to represent Him in matters such as this. As painful as these real-izations were, he felt good to sense a firm resolve within himself that he would never again allow himself to be so casual or disrespectful of the Lord's ordained representatives.

The Temptation to Delay

Christ has promised that "I, the Lord, forgive sins unto those who confess their sins before me and ask forgiveness, who have not sinned unto death" (D&C 64:7). When Satan finds us determined to do the *forsaking* part of repentance, he works hard to keep us from the *confessing* part, because he knows that without this vital part of repentance, we cannot be healed or cleansed.

> Our Father in Heaven knows how hard it is for you, and if you overcome your fear and take this action, he will bless you accordingly. Satan, of course, would love to have you postpone your confession indefinitely. *He'll whisper all manner of nonsense in your ear* about how the bishop may be shocked by your confession— or that the bishop would not be understanding—or that the bishop might not keep our confession confidential. ("Questions and Answers," *New Era*, Oct. 1989, 17; emphasis added)

Satan's power to "whisper" suggestions to our spirit minds is described in 2 Nephi 28:20–23. Drawing on these powers of decep-tion, the devil has developed endless schemes of rationalization to help us live a double life of hypocrisy, partially repenting while hiding our sins by avoiding confession. To sell us on his pseudo repentance—abandonment without confession—he may whisper things like: "Don't confess until after you've repented and it's all behind you." Or, "Go ahead and give it up if you must, but there is no need to humiliate yourself by confessing this before you repent and put it behind you. It will be less embarrassing to wait until some time has passed. Later, after you are all cleaned up, then you can make it known if you must, but for now, your life will be better if you keep this to yourself."

There is a vast difference in the results of merely *admitting* your mistake long after the fact, and honestly *confessing* your need for help and forgiveness while you are in the actual process of repenting. Satan uses this strategy because he knows that the longer we delay, the longer we will remain trapped in our sinful ways; the longer we delay, the weaker and more distant will be our relationship with Christ. He also knows that even if we do successfully *abandon* the sin, we can never find peace and forgiveness until we confess to the ones we have offended, and when appropriate, to our bishop or branch president. Trying to repent without confession is falling for Satan's fatal, going-only-part-of-the-way trap.

Confessing with Complete Honesty

"If we confess our sins, he is faithful and just to forgive us our sins, and to cleanse us from all unrighteousness." But, "If we say that we have no sin, we deceive ourselves, and the truth is not in us" (1 John 1:9, 8). Therefore, "He that covereth his sins shall not prosper: but whoso confesseth and forsaketh them shall have mercy" (Proverbs 28:13). To obtain that mercy we must make a full and honest confession, with no lingering secrets. Several years after publishing *The Miracle of Forgiveness,* President Kimball was still concerned about people not taking the confession part of repentance seriously. He lamented:

> Many people in their confession give only a skeleton picture and often rationalize and minimize the sins that have been done. . . . And so it is important that the one who is confessing should realize that the servant of the Lord to whom he makes bare his record represents the Lord. The Lord said again: "For he that receiveth my servants receiveth me, and he that receiveth me, receiveth my Father." And so a lie to an official of the Church who has a right to delve into our lives is tantamount to a lie to the Lord, and a half-truth to his officials is like a half-truth to the Lord, and rebellion against his leaders is comparable to rebellion against the Lord. ("What Is True Repentance?" *New Era,* May 1974, 7)

When we try to repent without a full and honest confession to those we have harmed or offended, and, in the case of major sins, to the Lord's priesthood representatives, the undisclosed sin rots and festers inside us like a spiritual cancer, spreading spiritual poison and preventing our spiritual recovery. President Spender W. Kimball compared this consequence to apples stored in a barrel. He explained:

> Thus one must not compromise or equivocate—he must make a clean, full confession. When the apples in a barrel rot, it is not enough to throw away half of the spoiled apples from the barrel and replace them with fresh apples on top. This would result in all the apples rotting. Instead it would be necessary to empty the barrel and completely clean and scrub—perhaps disinfect—the entire inside. Then the barrel could be safely filled

again with apples. Likewise in clearing up problems in our lives it
is well also to go to the bottom and confess all the transgressions
so that repentance begins with no half-truths, no pretense, no
unclean residue (*The Miracle of Forgiveness*, 180).

When we find ourselves hesitating to confess or feeling tempted
to minimize what we have done, we need to stand tall on the battle-
ground of repentance and "acknowledge [our] unworthiness before
God at all times" (Alma 38:14). The amazing and joyful truth is
that when we do confess our sins as He has commanded, the Lord
responds to our repentance much faster than He can when we
attempt to deny them or hide them.

Elder Curtis felt that he now had a clear vision of the mistakes of
the past and the path that beckoned him forward. He knelt in prayer
for several minutes, no longer pleading for direction or answers but
pouring out his gratitude to Heavenly Father for the Savior and His
Atonement and for the plan of happiness which he now knew was going
to return him to their presence.

Final Instructions

*R*eturning to the office, Elder Curtis opened the conversation by saying, "President Love, thank you for this article. I only wish I'd understood all of this back when I was dodging my responsibilities. And *opportunities*," he added hastily. "It was all so stupid," he said, "as if by not confessing, the Lord wouldn't know what I was inside. He knows everything about us, even our thoughts. Look, I found these two scriptures that explain how no one can hide their sins from God by not confessing."

He read to the president: " 'The eyes of the Lord are in every place, beholding the evil and the good' (Proverbs 15:3). And " 'Neither is there any creature that is not manifest in his sight: but all things are naked and opened unto the eyes of him with whom we have to do' (Hebrews 4:13)."

The president complimented him on his find. He said, "Elder Curtis, you weren't stupid, just lacking in understanding and conviction. Your two scriptures remind me of something I experienced many years ago. I had occasion to go into the restroom in a government building shortly after the law was passed that prohibited smoking anywhere in federal buildings. It had been my understanding that the law was not well received by many of their employees. And the moment I entered the restroom I could smell that someone was smoking in one of the stalls. I surmised that this man probably felt secure in the delusion that he was safe from detection because if no one could see him, then how would they know? Most likely, being a smoker, he was unaware of how easily that evidence was detectable to the nostrils of those who do not smoke.

"I appreciated his example, because it reminded me that many of us who commit sin are equally foolish in the assumption that, because we do it in secret, unseen by human eyes, we can get away with it undetected. How quickly we forget that no sin, or any other act for that matter, goes unnoticed by our God who knows all, sees all, and hears all. Alma reminded his son Corianton about this when he warned, 'Behold, ye cannot hide your crimes from God; and except ye repent they will stand as a testimony against you at the last day' (Alma 39:8).

The president continued, "I don't mean to make fun of the smoker. We've all done things like that. I remember something during my high school years that I am particularly embarrassed by. I did something that was wrong and reckless. I never got caught, but I never confessed it either, and it has bothered me all of these years."

The elder was interested and asked what he had done.

"Well, during the summer I was working for a farmer. One day, as we were working out in the fields, he needed me to drive back to the barn and get something. I was so excited when he told me to use his brand-new pickup. The truck had so much more power than my dad's old car. It had so much acceleration power that it actually pushed you back into the seat when you stomped on the accelerator pedal. I went faster and faster down the dirt road. What fun that was!

"Then, suddenly, I was faced with an unexpected ninety-degree turn. I slammed on the brakes and spun into the turn."

Elder Curtis leaned forward, intent on the story. "So what happened?" he asked. "Did you roll it?"

"No, I survived the turn without rolling the pickup or sliding into the ditch. I slid to a stop and boy was I scared. I got out to calm down and also to look around and see if anyone had seen what I had done. I didn't see anyone around, but I saw that I had left huge tracks in the gravel that would make my foolishness obvious to anyone going around this turn. Rather than being honest and telling the farmer, who employed me and trusted me with his valuable asset, how I had almost wrecked his truck, what I did was get a branch off a nearby bush and covered my tracks by sweeping the telltale ruts smooth. That way, I surmised, when the farmer drove through this same turn, he would not see the evidence of my risky maneuver.

"As I have grown older and wiser, I have learned that this kind of 'cover your tracks' substitute for repentance is what allows small sins to grow into critical issues that risk our marriages, family relationships, even our Church membership, and most certainly our eternal destiny. I think that is why Amulek emphasized that *now* is the time to repent. Take care of it at the beginning while things are small and more easily overcome, rather than later, when they have grown into monster habits and addictions, or even evil preferences (see Alma 34:31–35).

The president looked at his watch and said, "Elder Curtis, I've enjoyed my time with you these last two days, and I feel very encouraged by your spirit and your attitude. Elder Jones will be here anytime to get you. I need to leave right away for a meeting." Handing him some papers, he added, "I have one more article for you to study, but you can take it back to your apartment to do that. Are there any questions before I let you go?"

The Elder felt unnerved by the sudden end of something that had become very precious to him. "But, President," he stammered, "you haven't said what's to happen to me."

"Elder Curtis, you are in charge of what happens to you. Why would you expect me to decide that?"

The elder felt confused. He said, "Well, you're the president. I thought you would be my judge and tell me if I am to stay or to be sent home. Surely you can't mean that is up to me."

"No, I didn't mean that. It is not up to you alone. What I meant was about your repentance and your relationship to Heavenly Father. You are in charge of that regardless of what your leaders decide as to your status in the Church. I have discussed your situation with the Missionary Department in Salt Lake City, and they are in agreement with what *I* think we should do. But we need to know what *you* want to happen. So you go ahead with Elder Jones. It's only two days until zone conference. As you know, everyone will be having interviews with the president at that time. Let's plan for you to report to me at that time what you think should happen and then we'll decide. Are you okay with that?"

Suddenly the elder realized in a new way that it was time to stand on his own feet, to take responsibility and not depend on authority figures to tell him how to feel or every choice to make. He was dying to know what the president's decision was. But he was also excited to think that he could actually have a say that might affect the decision, because he already knew what he wanted to happen and how he was going to proceed. He smiled with relief and said, "Yes! I'm good to go and I'll be ready for that next interview."

But then he said, "What about my assignment to take Elder Brown's place?"

The president replied, "He's doing better and we expect him back on Monday. Thank you for helping with his duties, but now we need you back with Elder Jones."

Elder Curtis took the study papers, went upstairs, gathered his things, and brought them downstairs to the office. There was no sign of his companion, so he went and said good-bye to Sister Richardson, thanking her for all her help. As he left, she smiled with satisfaction at the new confidence she heard in his voice and the look of peace on his face.

Elder Curtis thought about reading the final article the president had just given him while he waited for Elder Jones, but he found he couldn't concentrate on it right now. He decided to wait until he was back at the apartment. He was tempted to at least peek at the title, curious what the president would have chosen for the final subject. But he decided against that because he knew he'd want to start reading. He gathered his things, deciding to wait for his companion in the front yard. It was only a couple of minutes before the three elders arrived. The other two were late for an appointment, so they dashed away without much conversation, leaving Elder Jones and Elder Curtis to themselves.

They felt awkward, not quite sure what to say or how much to say. It was uncharted territory. Elder Jones broke the ice by offering his hand. "Good to have you back," he said.

Elder Curtis replied, "It's good to be together again. I missed you." As they headed for the street, he asked, "Do we still have that appointment with Brother Nicolas tonight?

"No, his wife called and told me he slipped up again and not to come. Says he doesn't feel worthy to keep having us come over and teach when he hasn't kept his promise to stop smoking."

"That's great!" shouted Elder Curtis. "What an opportunity. I want to go see him anyway. I've got some good news to share that just might give him some encouragement."

"Well, all right," said Elder Jones in surprise, but with a big grin. "I'm anxious to hear this discussion myself."

Deciding to Be Chosen

*E*lder Jones was amazed by Brother Nicolas's change of attitude and obviously improved feelings of self-worth as Elder Curtis had taught him with passion and conviction. Then, after their first evening of working together, the two elders returned to their apartment. Elder Curtis immediately set about reading the last article that the president had given him that afternoon. He was intrigued by the title.

Deciding to Be Chosen

In an article about repentance, Elder Jay E. Jensen of the Seventy related that when he worked in the Missionary Department of the Church, the department was developing materials to help missionaries become better and do better. At that time one of the General Authorities shared the following experience, which teaches us that being accepted and chosen by God is a serious matter but is within the reach of every repentant person who sincerely seeks it. He shared:

> A little over a year ago, I had the privilege of interviewing a young man to go on a mission. Because he had committed a major transgression, it was necessary for him under then-existing policy to be interviewed by a General Authority. When the young man came in, I said, "Apparently there's been a major transgression

in your life, and that has necessitated this interview. Would you mind telling me what the problem was? What did you do?"

He laughed and said, "Well, there isn't anything I haven't done." I said, "Well, let's be more specific then. Have you . . . ?" And then this General Authority began to probe with some very specific questions. The young man laughed again and said, "I told you, I've done everything."

I said, "How many times have you . . ." He said very sarcastically, "Do you think I numbered them?" I said, "I would to God you could if you can't." He said, again quite sarcastically, "Well, I can't."

I said, "How about . . . ?" And then the General Authority probed in another direction. He said, "I told you. I've done everything." I said, "Drugs?" He said, "Yes," in a very haughty attitude. I said, *"What makes you think you're going on a mission then?"* He said, *"I know I'm going. My patriarchal blessing says I'll go on a mission, and I've repented. I haven't done any of those things for this past year. I have repented, and I know I'm going on a mission."*

I said, "My dear friend, I'm sorry but you are not going on a mission. Do you think we could send you out with those clean, wholesome young men who have never violated the code? Do you think we could have you go out and boast and brag about your past? *You haven't repented; you have just stopped doing something.*

"Sometime in your life you need to visit Gethsemane; and when you have been there, you'll understand what repentance is. Only after you have suffered in some small degree as the Savior suffered in Gethsemane will you know what repentance is. The Savior has suffered in a way none of us understands for every transgression committed. How dare you laugh and jest and have a haughty attitude about your repentance? I'm sorry, you are not going on a mission."

He started to cry, and he cried for several minutes. I didn't say a word. Finally, he said, "I guess that's the first time I have cried since I was five years old." I said, "If you had cried like that the first time you were tempted to violate the moral code, you possibly would be going on a mission."

He left the office, and I think he felt I was really cruel. I explained to the bishop and the stake president that the boy could not go on a mission. (Elder Vaughn J. Featherstone, Sweden Area Conference, Youth Session, Aug. 1974; as quoted by Elder Jay E. Jensen, in "Do You Know How to Repent?" *New Era*, Nov. 1999, 5–6; emphasis added)

Elder Curtis paused to consider how this was exactly what he had expected to happen to him had he told the truth during his worthiness interviews. He wondered how his life might have been different if he'd had the courage to confess back then instead of now. He felt ashamed as he remembered President Kimball's description of those who pretend to repent with nothing but "a brushing-off gesture" (*The Miracle of Forgiveness*, 15). He was anxious to find out what happened to this young man, now judged unworthy of being chosen. He continued reading.

> Elder Jensen continued the General Authority's account; he related, "About six months later the same General Authority returned to that city to speak in a lecture series held in the evening. When he finished, many young adults lined up to shake hands with him. As he shook hands, one by one, he looked up and saw the young man that he had previously interviewed standing in the line about four back." He then gave the rest of the General Authority's story:
>
>> My mind quickly flashed back to our interview. I recalled his laughing and haughty attitude. I remembered how sarcastic he was. Pretty soon he was right in front of me. I was on the stand bending over, and as I reached down to shake his hand, I noticed a great change had taken place. He had tears in his eyes. He had almost a holy glow about his countenance. He took my hand in his and said, "I've been there; I've been to Gethsemane and back." I said, "I know. It shows in your face."
>
> The General Authority concluded his account: "We can be forgiven for our transgressions, *but we must understand that just to stop doing something is not repentance.* If it had not been for the Savior and the miracle of forgiveness, this young man would have carried his transgressions throughout all eternity. We ought to love the Savior and serve Him for this reason and this reason alone" (Elder Vaughn J. Featherstone, Sweden Area Conference, Youth Session, Aug. 1974; as quoted by Elder Jay E. Jensen, in "Do You Know How to Repent?" *New Era*, Nov. 1999, 6; emphasis added).

Had he read this account two days ago, Elder Curtis would have been amazed at the mercy and forgiveness shown to this wayward elder. But now he understood that God has both the power and the determination to rescue, change, save, and exalt every person who is willing to be changed and chosen. He thought about examples in the scriptures of men of God who had been just as bad if not worse than the young man just described. He remembered that Alma and the four sons of Mosiah, before their repentance, had been described as "the vilest of sinners" (Mosiah 28:4). They had not only sought personal pleasure in sin but had actually sought to destroy the Church. So had Paul, who was also an enemy to the Christians and had been responsible for the death and imprisonment of many disciples (see Acts 8:3; 9:1; 22:4).

He opened his scriptures and read what had now become one of his favorite verses. "For the natural man is an enemy to God, and has been from the fall of Adam, and will be, forever and ever, unless he *yields to the enticings of the Holy Spirit,* and putteth off the natural man and becometh a saint through the Atonement of Christ the Lord, and becometh as a child, submissive, meek, humble, patient, full of love, willing to submit to all things which the Lord seeth fit to inflict upon him, even as a child doth submit to his father" (Mosiah 3:19; emphasis added).

He knew that the young man in the story had ceased to be "an enemy to God" when he surrendered his nature to "the enticings of the Holy Spirit" and allowed Christ's Atonement to make a new person of him. Elder Curtis felt the same invitation beckoning him. He rejoiced because he now knew that only those who refuse to change will remain enemies to God. And he knew in his heart that this process of change was also happening in his own life. He continued reading.

> We can learn more about the process of being chosen from Orson F. Whitney, who was ordained an apostle in 1906, but who, years before, had a rather poor start on his first mission. In Oct. of 1876 at the age of twenty-one, he was called to labor in Pennsylvania. He was not particularly interested in religion and gave the following reasons for why he felt poorly prepared to preach:
>
>> Up to this time I had bent most of my energies in the direction of music and the drama, which I dearly loved. I had no desire to be a writer or a public speaker, and did not dream that I could make any mark either in literature or in oratory. Still less did I imagine that I was destined to become a preacher of the gospel. As a child I was religiously inclined, though I revolted to some extent against religious discipline. As a youth I became indifferent to spiritual things, though at the same time I led a moral life. (*LDS Biographical Encyclopedia,* 659)
>
> After serving a few months in Pennsylvania, he began touring some of the major historical sights and sending his impressions back to Salt Lake City, which were well received in one of its newspapers. He was not really committed to the mission "and he candidly

confesses that he was then more interested in his newspaper correspondence than in the labors of the ministry" (*LDS Biographical Encyclopedia*, 660). After returning to the mission from his touring, he was given a dream that changed his spiritual priorities, helped him to repent, and led him into a life that would make it possible to become chosen. Of this dream he related:

> I thought I was in the garden of Gethsemane, a witness of the Savior's agony. I seemed to be standing behind a tree in the foreground of the picture, from which point I could see without being seen. The Savior, with the Apostles Peter, James and John, entered the garden through a little wicket gate at my right, where he stationed them in a group, telling them to pray. He then passed over to my left, but still in front of me, where he knelt and prayed also. His face, which was towards me, streamed with tears, as he besought the Father to let the cup pass, and added, "not my will but thine be done."
>
> Having finished his prayer, he arose and crossed to where the Apostles were kneeling fast asleep. He shook them gently, they awoke and he reproved them for their apathy. Again he bade them pray, and again crossed to his place and prayed, returning as before to find them sleeping. This happened three times, until I was perfectly familiar with his face, form and movements. He was much taller than ordinary men, and though meek, far more dignified than any being I had ever beheld; and he wore a look of ineffable tenderness and compassion, even while reproving His disciples. My heart went out to him as never before to anybody or to anything; I loved him with all my soul. I wept at seeing him weep, and felt for him the deepest sympathy.
>
> Then of a sudden the circumstances changed, though the scene remained the same. Instead of before the crucifixion, it was after. The Savior and the three Apostles, whom he had beckoned to him, now stood in a group at the left, and were about to take their departure, ascending into heaven. I could endure it no longer, but rushed out from behind the tree, fell at his feet, clasped him around the knees and begged him to take me also.
>
> With a look of infinite tenderness, as of a father or an elder brother, he stooped, lifted me up and embraced me, saying as he did so in the kindest and gentlest manner possible, while slowly shaking his head and sweetly smiling, "No, my son, these can go with me; for they have finished their work; but you must stay and finish yours!" Still I clung to him, and the contact was so real that I felt the warmth of his bosom as I rested upon it. Gazing up into his face, I once more besought him, "Well, promise me that I will come to you at the last." Again he smiled sweetly, and

there was a look as if he would have gladly granted my request had it been wise to do so. He then said, *"That will depend entirely upon yourself."*

I awoke with a sob, and it was morning. This dream made a wonderful impression upon me, paving the way to my thorough conversion, which soon followed. Among the things it taught me was not to sleep at my post, and to regard first the duties of my mission, and not allow anything to interfere with them. (*LDS Biographical Encyclopedia*, 660–61; emphasis added).

We learn from this account that being chosen for the celestial kingdom is not based upon luck, like a lottery, but upon faithfulness and obedience to our covenants. We do not have to hold our breath, as it were, hoping that God will choose us at the last day. If we wish to remain chosen, we must do the proper choosing now, while there is time to prepare.

The Savior's love and forgiveness are bigger than any fault of which we are repentant. Our value to Him is priceless. He left His throne of glory to suffer and die for us, to prepare the way and make it possible for every person who wants to return to Heavenly Father to do so. God wants every person to be chosen, "for there is no respect of persons with God" (Romans 2:11), and "he inviteth them all to come unto him and partake of his goodness; and he denieth none that come unto him . . . and all are alike unto God" (2 Nephi 26:33).

Many people, however, are living in hopeless despair. They feel their lives are broken and ruined beyond repair, like the broken tree shown below. But when I look at this picture, I don't see misfortune or hopelessness. What I see is a perfect symbol for the infinite power of the Savior to restore broken lives. This symbol reminds me that it is impossible for any person or any situation to ever fall beyond the power of Christ's grace and healing. No situation of sin, addiction, or heartache is ever beyond His power to restore life, peace, happiness, and self-respect—in other words, wholeness and well-being.

As Mormon emphasized, "We see that *whosoever will* may lay hold upon the word of God, which is quick and powerful, which shall divide asunder all the cunning and the snares and the wiles of the devil, and lead the man of Christ in a strait and narrow course across that everlasting gulf of misery which is prepared to engulf the wicked—And land their souls, yea, their immortal souls, at the right hand of God in the kingdom of heaven, to sit down with Abraham, and Isaac, and with Jacob, and with all our holy fathers, to go no more out" (Helaman 3:29–30; emphasis added).

However, we are not chosen merely to enter His kingdom and "sit down with" the prophets. As wonderful as it will be to mingle with them, the Lord has much bigger things in mind for His chosen. At that far and distant day of fulfillment, when God has finished His perfecting work within us, He means for us to spend the rest of eternity assisting in His work to embody and glory our own continuing posterity (see D&C 132 and the following chapter.)

There were tears in Elder Curtis's eyes as he finished reading. He felt his heart swelling as the Spirit witnessed that all he had read applied to him, as well as every other child of God. He stood and searched through the desk. He found some stamps and envelopes and a note pad. He knelt in a heartfelt prayer of gratitude and commitment. Then he sat down to write three letters: one to his parents, one to his bishop, and one to his stake president.

Rising above Perfectionism

*T*wo days later, all the missionaries in Elder Curtis's area gathered for zone conference. After the preliminaries were completed, the president stood to teach. Elder Curtis was so anxious to learn what his decision was that he wished they could skip this part and get right to his interview, but he resigned himself to the delay, glad to learn more from the president.

"Elders and Sisters, thank you for coming today. Sister Love and I know that you love the people you serve. We know that you pray for them and yearn to share the joys of the gospel with them. I commend you for that. I appreciate you and thank you for all that you do and for all that you strive to do. The Lord loves you. I testify that He is always mindful of your desires, your discouragements, and your efforts to be faithful.

"Our training this morning is not going to cover the missionary skills that we normally discuss. Instead, we are going to focus on the improvement of personal discipleship. To teach by the Spirit, we must be worthy of the Spirit. For that reason, if we are seriously lacking in our personal discipleship, we will not be truly successful as missionaries—or in any other calling—no matter how skillful we are.

"We are all under obligation to seek perfection, but it is not appropriate to try so hard that we become obsessed with this quest or to feel that anything less than perfect is unacceptable. As members of Christ's Church, we have already been called to prepare ourselves for exaltation in the celestial kingdom. You must understand that if you keep your temple covenants to the best of your ability, even though you are less than perfect in doing so, you will become the kind of person who qualifies to be chosen.

"You should all have received printed handouts containing the quotations from the brethren and the scriptures that I am going to use. You are welcome to follow along with me, and I would encourage you to make notes on your handouts as we go."

Elder Curtis smiled inwardly, wondering how the other missionaries would feel if they knew what a treasure of similar handouts he now possessed. It didn't even occur to him that they would be curious as to how he got them.

The president continued. "We are going to start our discussion with four important quotes about the subject of guilt. I have noticed a peculiar phenomenon in the Church that, in many cases, the more active and valiant a person is in the gospel, the more guilty they may feel about the mission of seeking perfection. As well intended as such feelings may be, they are not productive, nor are they pleasing to the Lord. It concerns me when I see you trying so hard and then failing to give yourself credit. Elder Cecil O. Samuelson of the Seventy expressed this concern better than I can say it. He observed: 'For over twenty years I was a professor and practitioner of medicine, and I have a concern that I know is shared by other General Authorities. A matter of great concern for some of you is the issue that mental health professionals describe as "perfectionism." There is an understandable goal to follow the Savior's direction to "be ye therefore perfect" (Matthew 5:48). While this goal is admirable and appropriate, *it is unfortunate that some consider that this perfection must occur immediately.*'[1]

"The second quotation comes from Elder Marvin J. Ashton, who expressed similar concern when he said, 'We need to come to terms with our desire to reach perfection and our frustration when our accomplishments or behaviors are less than perfect. *I feel that one of the great myths we would do well to dispel is that we've come to earth to perfect ourselves, and nothing short of that will do.* If I understand the teachings of the prophets of this dispensation correctly, we will not become perfect in this life, though we can make significant strides toward that goal."[2]

"Boyd K. Packer commented: 'Some worry endlessly over missions that were missed, or marriages that did not turn out, or babies that did not arrive, or children that seem lost, or dreams unfulfilled, or because age limits what they can do. *I do not think it pleases the Lord when we worry because we think we never do enough or that what we do is never good enough.*'[3]

"Our fourth quote is from Patricia Holland, wife of Elder Jeffrey R. Holland, who also had some strong words on this issue. She reflected:

> I think that the Lord will not be particularly comfortable dwelling with a person who (to the exclusion of all other joys and blessings in life) ponders continually on his or her problems, who is obsessed and finally immobilized by them, who hasn't learned to bear those limitations serenely. That isn't humility, it is near-blasphemy. When you dwell on your limitations excessively, to the point that they affect your inner view and strength, you mock God in his very creation. You deny the divinity within you. You resist the gift of Christ on the cross. So be patient in your pursuit of perfection.[4]

Elder Curtis wondered what it would be like to worry over minor imperfections instead of being preoccupied with guilt from past sin. He was glad to be putting the sinful memories of his life in the past and moving forward into a joyful life of faithful discipleship.

"Now, Elders and Sisters, it is easy to understand why so many of us get trapped by feelings of falling short, because we all know how far we are from the goal of perfection. I love the assuring words of Elder Neal A. Maxwell on this. He counseled: 'Now may I speak, not to the slackers in the kingdom, but to those who carry their own load and more; not to those lulled into false security, but to those buffeted by false insecurity, who, though laboring devotedly in the Kingdom, have recurring feelings of falling forever short. Earlier disciples who heard Jesus preach some exacting doctrines were also anxious and said, 'Who then can be saved?' (Mark 10:26). *The first thing to be said of this feeling of inadequacy is that it is normal.*' He concluded, 'There is no way the Church can honestly describe where we must yet go and what we must yet do without creating a sense of immense distance.'[5]

"Let's not fall into the trap that Sister Holland warned us about. We are all human. We are all mortal. We are all living in a fallen world and trying to overcome our fallen natures. As Elder Marvin J. Ashton advised, 'Somehow we need to bridge the gap between continually striving to improve and yet not feeling defeated when our actions aren't perfect all the time.'[6] Many of you have expressed these very concerns in our interviews, and I hate to see you impose unnecessary guilt and burdens upon yourselves when you are doing so well in the eyes of the Lord. This feeling of inadequacy is a challenge faced by every worthy member, and so we hope that our discussion today will help you to bridge this gap. One thing that helps me to cross that bridge is remembering that as high as the standards are for a temple recommend, those questions only pertain to our *worthiness*. There is no inquiry as to our present level of perfection. Elder Marvin J. Ashton taught, 'Worthiness is a process, and perfection is an eternal trek. We can be worthy to enjoy certain privileges without being perfect.'[7]

What does perfection mean?

As the president looked over the group, his heart was filled with love for the goodness he saw in them. He continued.

"Just what did the Savior have in mind when He commanded us to become perfect? He said, 'I have given you an example, that ye should do as I have done to you,' and 'He that believeth on me, the works that I do shall he do also' (John 13:15; 14:12). After lunch we will have further discussion on what it actually means to do as the Savior has done. We will also learn some practical ways that we can go about doing that. In the meantime, as we discuss seeking perfection, I want you to be aware of a trap. The trap I refer to is the mistake of substituting *doing* for *being*.

"We mortals tend to measure success and achievement with a checklist of things that can be seen—things that we have *done*, or accomplished. And I'm not saying that that is bad. Actually, I think it is important and helpful. But the emphasis in our quest for perfection should be about who and what we are *becoming* more than it is on the outward appearance of our actions. I would like you to keep in mind that while the things we must do to obey the commandments are important, and while they do provide a path to our becoming, they are never an end unto themselves.

"Nephi stressed just how important it is to follow the Savior's example so that we may become like Him. He emphasized that 'unless a man shall endure to the end, in following the example of the Son of the living God, he cannot be saved' (2 Nephi 31:16). After His resurrection, the Savior asked: 'Therefore, what manner of men ought ye to be?' His answer was, 'Verily I say unto you, even as I am' (3 Nephi 27:27). He also challenged: 'I would that ye should be perfect even as I, or your Father who is in heaven is perfect' (3 Nephi 12:48)."

The president noticed that some of the missionaries were squirming uncomfortably in their chairs. Sometimes those verses made him uncomfortable too.

A sister missionary raised her hand and said, "President, you shared some quotes that said we don't have to become perfect here in this life. But I didn't hear any such qualifications in the Savior's words that you just quoted. It sounds like He was saying that we should become perfect now, here in this life. If that is true, then it's pretty discouraging, because I don't know anyone that I would consider perfect, and I don't see how that is even possible in this world."

Her question made Elder Curtis feel uncomfortable. It was easy to see how such a question might throw the president off of his planned presentation, but as he glanced at the next part of his handout, he realized he should have known better. The answer to her question (which he figured was shared by most of the missionaries) was right there as the very next subject.

After thanking the sister for her concern, the President said, "I think we all have some of those same concerns. So will your investigators, who may easily feel overwhelmed as they learn all that it means to become a member of the Church. Let's see if we find some answers in the next section on your handouts." He continued.

"Elders and Sisters, I understand how incredible this invitation seems, how impossible and unreachable. Considering our mortal limitations, attaining perfection in this life can seem so unthinkably impossible that we may question if the scriptures really mean what it sounds like they said. But I bear you witness that they do. During a discussion on this very subject in a training session with Church Educational System teachers in Salt Lake City, Utah, Elder Bruce R. McConkie testified: 'Our God, who is triumphant in all battles against the forces of evil, will surely be victorious in the numbers of his children who will be saved.' "[8]

The president looked directly at the sister who had asked the question. He smiled at her as he said, "Most of the commandments that we deal with in our daily lives pertain to how we live our lives right here and now. But it was not God's intent for us to feel inadequate or overwhelmed by this staggering invitation. Let's consider some of the other revelations on this subject and see if we can agree on a reasonable time frame to fulfill this commandment.

"Paul taught that one of the reasons Christ gave us priesthood leaders and a Church organization is 'for the perfecting of the saints, for the work of the ministry, for the edifying of the body of Christ.' And then he described the ultimate goal of that process of edifying and perfecting. He said that this work would continue until 'we all come in the unity of the faith, and of the knowledge of the Son of God, unto a perfect man.' He then gave us a definition of perfection as attaining '*unto the measure of the stature of the fulness of Christ*' (Ephesians 4:12–13; emphasis added). Paul also reported: 'The Spirit itself beareth witness with our spirit, that we are the children of God: And if children, then heirs; heirs of God, and *joint-heirs with Christ*; if so be that we suffer with him, that we may be also *glorified together*' (Romans 8:16–17; emphasis added). Elders and Sisters, what do you think it would mean to be a joint heir with Christ and to be glorified with Him? And is this something we would expect to happen in this life, or are we now being given glimpses into eternity?

"The answer to that question was revealed to Joseph Smith. He taught that those who inherit the highest degree in the celestial kingdom will be exalted and become gods. He said first: 'And then shall the angels be crowned with the glory of his might, and the saints shall be filled with his glory, and receive their inheritance *and be made equal with him*' (D&C 88:107; emphasis added). This stunning revelation was later expanded with greater detail. Those so exalted, it states,

> . . . shall inherit thrones, kingdoms, principalities, and powers, dominions, all heights and depths . . . and they shall pass by the angels, and the gods, which are set there, to their exaltation and glory in all things, as hath been sealed upon their heads, which glory shall be a fulness and a continuation of the seeds forever and ever. Then shall they be gods, because they have no end; therefore shall they be from everlasting to everlasting, because they continue; then shall they be above all, because all things are subject unto them.

Then shall they be gods, because they have all power, and the angels are subject unto them. (D&C 132:19–20)

"Of course, none of this would be possible without the help of our Savior. As we struggle to grasp the actual possibility of such a duty and destiny, we must nourish our faith and expectations with the assurance that 'the Lord giveth no commandments [or invitations] unto the children of men, save he shall *prepare a way* for them that they may accomplish the thing which he hath commanded them' (1 Nephi 3:7; emphasis added). Elder Neal A. Maxwell's words also nourish our faith in this challenge. Referring to verses like Matthew 5:48 which command us to become 'perfect even as your Father in Heaven is perfect,' he asked: 'Would a Lord who cannot lie taunt us with any possibility that is irrevocably out of our reach?'[9]

Boundaries and Mind-set

"Some of our misunderstanding of this lofty destiny comes from not realizing that there are two kinds of perfection. The first is called finite, which is limited but achievable in some aspects of mortal life. The second and most important is the infinite, or eternal perfection that will only be achieved in the eternities to come.[10] So Elders and Sisters, let me invite you to think about seeking perfection in several different ways. Before an artist sets about to create a picture, he must first determine how large he means for it to be, because, when it is done, it will be confined within the size of the framework chosen to border the picture. You cannot start drawing or painting a six-inch picture and then later expect to expand it into a four-foot square. You must have the end in mind before you begin."

Warming to the subject, he continued: "Coaches apply the same principle. As they train their athletes, they tell them about the records of past achievements, like the highest jump, the longest jump, the fastest race, and so forth. They do this to form a mind-set that will open mental boundaries and possibilities without limitations. They are striving to set benchmarks for possible achievement that give us permission to expand our vision and expectations beyond those of the past. For a long time, runners had the limiting mind-set that running a mile race took more than four minutes. But once Roger Bannister broke that record, many others were able to follow his example.

"Motivators say things like 'Reach for the stars' or 'Lengthen your stride' to open our minds to possibilities that have no unnecessary borders or limitations. Sometimes we are frustrated by motivators who say things like: 'Whether you think you can or think you can't, you are right.' But like it or not, it is a fact that our attitudes and beliefs about what we conceive as realistic expectations will put boundaries on what we can achieve. And so we should be grateful for prophets and priesthood leaders who, like coaches and other mentors, have a higher vision than we do, and who help us to reach further than we might otherwise.

"I believe that is what Christ was trying to do for us when He said, 'I would that ye should be perfect even as I, or your Father who is in heaven is perfect' (3 Nephi 12:48). It was not a commandment for immediate achievement but an invitation to look into the eternities and see eventual possibilities. He gave this amazing invitation to give us a divine mind-set—a direction and a destination toward which we should set our eternal goals as we continue to improve throughout our mortal probation."

Elder Curtis remembered about how panicked he had been a few days ago, and how carefully the president had helped him raise his desires and goals.

Perfecting Beyond the Veil

"This is how the prophet Joseph described the progressive, incremental process of growing into perfection. 'When you climb up a ladder, you must begin at the bottom, and ascend step by step, until you arrive at the top and so it is with the principles of the Gospel—you must begin with the first, and go on until you learn all the principles of exaltation.' Then he added the caution that completing this process will extend into the eternities. *'But it will be a great while after you have passed through the veil before you will have learned them. It is not all to be comprehended in this world; it will be a great work to learn our salvation and exaltation even beyond the grave.'*[11]

"President Joseph Fielding Smith added to our understanding of Joseph's words. He observed: 'I believe the Lord meant just what he said: that we should be perfect, as our Father in heaven is perfect (see Matt. 5:48 and 3 Nephi 12:48). That will not come all at once, but line upon line, and precept upon precept, example upon example, *and even then not as long as we live in this mortal life, for we will have to go even beyond the grave before we reach that perfection and shall be like God.'*[12]

Elder Bruce R. McConkie's teachings on this subject can also help us to overcome our worries about not being good enough soon enough. He explains that all that is required of a temple-attending member to be accepted and chosen for exaltation is a reasonable and sincere effort to do our best. There is no justification for a radical extremism that demands more perfection than is reasonable in a fallen world.

> We don't need to get a complex or get a feeling that you have to be perfect to be saved. You don't. There's only been one perfect person, and that's the Lord Jesus, but in order to be saved in the Kingdom of God and in order to pass the test of mortality, what you have to do is get on the straight and narrow path—thus charting a course leading to eternal life—and then, being on that path, pass out of this life in full fellowship.
>
> I'm not saying that you don't have to keep the commandments. I'm saying you don't have to be perfect to be saved. If you did, no one would be saved. The way it operates is this: you get on the path that's named the "straight and narrow." You do it by entering the gate of repentance and baptism. The straight and narrow path leads from the gate of repentance and baptism, a very great distance, to a reward that's called eternal life.
>
> You don't have to do what Jacob said, "Go beyond the mark." You don't have to live a life that's truer than true. You don't have to have an excessive zeal that becomes fanatical and becomes unbalancing. What you have to do is stay in the mainstream of the Church—keeping the commandments, paying your tithing, serving in the organizations of the Church, loving the Lord, staying on the straight and narrow path.
>
> If you're on that path when death comes—because this is the time and the day appointed, this [is] the probationary estate—you'll never fall off from it, and, for all practical purposes, your calling and election is made sure. Now, that isn't the definition of that term, but the end result will be the same.[13]

Obtaining Perfection Is a Gradual Process

"The Lord said, 'I will give unto you a pattern in all things, that ye may not be deceived' (D&C 52:14). One of the most valuable 'patterns' He has given us is that achievement and growth come through a process of gradual steps, over time, rather than in huge and sudden leaps. He gave this pattern in the way He created our world. The scriptures show that He did not do that in one session but divided His labors into progressive steps. We are expected to apply the same pattern in our process of personal development. Elder Merrill J. Bateman of the Seventy reminded us of this principle when he taught:

> The second step along Mormon's path of discipleship is to "lay hold upon every good thing," to incorporate sacred truths into our lives. This involves faith, repentance, participation in sacred covenants, companionship of the Holy Spirit, and enduring to the end. *It does not mean laying hold on every good thing all at once.* The principle is "line upon line, precept upon precept, here a little and there a little" (2 Nephi 28:30).[14]

Elder Joseph B. Wirthlin also addressed this principle when he stated:

> Our Heavenly Father loves each one of us and understands that this process of climbing higher takes preparation, time, and commitment. He understands that we will make mistakes at times, that we will stumble, that we will become discouraged and perhaps even wish to give up and say to ourselves it is not worth the struggle.
>
> An eternal principle is revealed in holy writ: "It is not requisite that a man should run faster than he has strength. And again, it is expedient that he should be diligent, that thereby he might win the prize" (Mosiah 4:27).
>
> We don't have to be fast; we simply have to be steady and move in the right direction. We have to do the best we can, one step after another.[15]

"Elder Dean L. Larsen of the Seventy also warned about being overanxious. He cautioned: 'Trying to measure up to too many particular expectations without some sense of self-tolerance can cause spiritual and emotional "burnout." '[16] We are all anxious to increase our abilities to serve and keep our covenants, and that is good, as long as we remember the line-upon-line principle and do not diminish our productivity by unrealistically expecting more of ourselves than God does. This necessitates the discipline of patience with ourselves as we make attempts to do well, perform less than we intended, repent, regroup, and retry. Elder Maxwell taught: 'The gospel suggests to us ultimate perfection, but eternal progression rests on the assumption of gradual but regular improvement in our lives. In the city of Enoch the near perfection of this people occurred "in the process of time" over many, many years. This is also the case with us."[17]

"The Savior showed His acceptance of this incremental process of growth when He stated: 'Ye must practise virtue and holiness before me continually' (D&C 46:33). The word *practise* shows that God is allowing us time to learn and grow and that He does not expect immediate perfection in everything. After lunch we will discuss the process that the Lord has provided for seeking to emulate His divine character and perfection in our daily lives."

The president was pleased to see that the missionaries were sitting more relaxed now. He knew that the next section would provide them with even more confidence in their ability to meet the Savior's expectations.

Avoiding Discouragement by Accepting Small Steps

"Elder Maxwell advised that, 'It is good to remember how young we are spiritually.'[18] In the eternal scheme of things, we are still in kindergarten. The coach who tries to inspire his athletes with world records never intends for them to go into spasms of self-condemnation for failing to measure up to those standards of achievement as they begin their training. Likewise, the Savior never intended His invitation toward future perfection to inflict hang-ups or self-condemnation for our present imperfections.

"It is unrealistic to expect a sudden leap from a telestial level of behavior to a celestial level. Because we are mortal and fallen, this process will involve many cycles of failure and repentance. In our eagerness to please the Lord, we must not expect too much of ourselves too soon and then fall into discouragement or depression because we are not perfect as quickly as we had hoped to be. I am so grateful that Elder Joseph B. Wirthlin affirmed: 'We don't have to be perfect today. We don't have to be better than someone else. All we have to do is to be the very best we can.'[19] His words remind me of the frequent encouragements that President Hinckley gives in his talks. For example, 'Now, brethren and sisters, let us return to our homes with resolution in our hearts to do a little better than we have done in the past. We can all be a little kinder, a little more generous, a little more thoughtful of one another.'[20]

"As we strive to improve and perfect ourselves, it is wise to remember that the Lord said, 'Ye are not able to abide the presence of God now, neither the ministering of angels; wherefore, continue in patience until ye are perfected' (D&C 67:13). President Ezra Taft Benson spoke of this patience when he commented: 'The Lord is pleased with every effort, even the tiny, daily ones in which we strive to be more like Him. Though we may see that we have far to go on the road to perfection, we must not give up hope.'[21]

"Elders and Sisters, it seems to me that if God is willing to accept our best efforts, even though less than perfect, if He does not reject nor condemn us for having unconquered weaknesses as we continue to work out our salvation, then we ought not to condemn our imperfections while we are in the process of learning to overcome them. As Elder Neal A. Maxwell pointed out, 'Our perfect Father does not expect us to be perfect children yet. He had only one such Child. Meanwhile, therefore, sometimes with smudges on our cheeks, dirt on our hands, and shoes untied, stammeringly but smilingly we present God with a dandelion—as if it were an orchid or a rose! If for now the dandelion is the best we have to offer, He receives it, knowing what we may later place on the altar.'[22] "

Elder Curtis passed a note to his companion, recommending that it might be helpful to share some of these ideas with their investigator who has been feeling bad about not being good enough to be baptized yet.

The President concluded: "All right, Elders and Sisters, enough said on all that. It is probably more than you ever wanted to hear, but it is what you needed to hear. Let's have our closing prayer and blessing on the food. Then, after lunch, we'll reassemble and learn what to do in our day-to-day pursuit of perfection."

As they went to lunch, Elder Curtis found himself repenting of his previous impatience. He was very thankful to have received this important perspective and was anxious to see how the president would reduce such lofty goals to a practical, day-to-day process. Although still anxious for his interview, he was excited to hear the remainder of the president's teachings.

Notes

1 "What Does It Mean to Be Perfect?" *New Era*, Jan. 2006, 10; emphasis added.

2 "On Being Worthy," *Ensign*, May 1989, 20; emphasis added.

3 "The Least of These," *Ensign*, Nov. 2004, 86; emphasis added.

4 "Be Renewed in the Spirit of your Mind," *BYU Devotional Speeches of the Year*, 6 Sept. 1988, 25.

5 "Notwithstanding My Weakness," *Ensign*, Nov. 1976, 12; emphasis added.

6 "On Being Worthy," *Ensign*, May 1989, 20.

7 Ibid.

8 *Are We There Yet?*, 10.

9 *The Neal A. Maxwell Quote Book*, 244.

10 See Elder Bruce R. McConkie, *Mormon Doctrine*, 567.

11 *Teaching of the Prophet Joseph Smith*, 348; emphasis added.

12 *Doctrines of Salvation*, 2:18–19; emphasis added.

13 "The Probationary Test of Mortality," Devotional Address given at the University of Utah Institute of Religion, 10 Jan. 1982, 12–13; emphasis added.

14 "Becoming a Disciple of Christ," *Ensign*, Apr. 2006, 16; emphasis added.

15 "One Step after Another," *Ensign*, Nov. 2001, 25.

16 "The Peaceable Things of the Kingdom," *New Era*, Feb. 1986, 6.

17 *The Neal A. Maxwell Quote Book*, 244.

18 Ibid., 243.

19 "One Step after Another," *Ensign*, Nov. 2001, 25.

20 "Thanks to the Lord for His Blessings," *Ensign*, May 1999, 88.

21 "A Mighty Change of Heart," *Ensign*, Oct. 1989, 2.

22 *The Neal A. Maxwell Quote Book*, 243.

The Path to Perfection

The missionaries gathered after lunch. Handouts were distributed and many of the missionaries opened notebooks, including Elder Curtis, who was anxious for any instructions on what how to better his life.

After the hymn and prayer, President Love began. "Elders and Sisters, this morning we learned about striving toward perfection, but without burdening ourselves with premature or unreasonable expectations. However, there was one thing we did not do, and that was to make a list of all the commandments we are required to keep in order to be perfect." Some of the missionaries squirmed uncomfortably, dreading what they thought might be coming next. President Love smiled, knowing the simplicity of what was to follow and continued.

"How many commandments do you think we need to put on that list?" Answering the question himself, he explained: "If it were possible to make such a list, it would be very, very long because to become perfect, we would have to obey *every* commandment perfectly. That seems overwhelming! Fortunately, our quest to attain perfection is much simpler than complying with such a long checklist.

"Let me remind you of something. During His earthly ministry,

Jesus was challenged to specify which, out of all the commandments, was the greatest or most important. His answer was, 'Thou shalt love the Lord thy God with all thy heart, and with all thy soul, and with all thy mind.' He then emphasized, 'This is the first and great commandment. And the second is like unto it, Thou shalt love thy neighbour as thyself.' The Savior then added, 'On these two commandments hang all the law and the prophets' (Matthew 22:37–40). In another account He said. 'There is none other commandment greater than these' (Mark 12:31).

"Based on those statements, Paul summarized: 'Now the end of the commandment is charity' (1 Timothy 1:5), and 'All the law is fulfilled in one word, even in this; Thou shalt love thy neighbour as thyself' (Galatians 5:14). We find the same emphasis in the Book of Mormon. For example, Nephi said that 'the Lord God hath given a commandment that all men should have charity, which charity is love. And except they should have charity they were nothing' (2 Nephi 26:30). So, as important as good works are in serving each other and in building the kingdom, in one sense we could say that all of the rules and commandments in the gospel are but scaffolding to train us to love and care and serve in the way that God does."

One of the sisters raised her hand. When the president called on her she said, "President, I'm sorry to interrupt when you've just begun, but I thought perfection meant keeping all the commandments."

President Love explained: "It does mean that, but feeling and giving love is the best way to keep the commandments. Remember from our discussion this morning that perfection is more about what we *are* than what we *do*. This may surprise you, but in the scriptures, charity 'is never used to denote alms or deeds or benevolence.'[1] If we have charity, then of course we will keep the commandments and do good things for others, including charitable things.

"The point is that the more one loves God and others, or in other words, the more charity we have, the less we need rules and commandments to govern our behavior. When we are possessed of charity, we will do kind and loving things toward others, not because it is commanded of us, but because it is what we are, and because we become incapable of acting toward others in any other manner. Accordingly, charity is much more than doing good deeds; it is becoming like Christ. You see, God does not treat us in a kind, patient, and merciful way because he *has* love, but because 'God *is* love' (1 John 4:8, 16;

emphasis added). And obtaining the gift of charity is the most direct path to becoming a Christlike person—one who loves and cares and serves others in the way the Savior does."

The thoughts of every missionary in the room turned to the people they had learned to love as they served and taught them on their missions. Many of the missionaries realized how much more they had learned about love through their experiences of selfless service.

The president seemed to reflect for a moment, and then he said, "Let me explain it this way. When the Savior said, 'A new commandment I give unto you, That ye love one another; as I have loved you, that ye also love one another' (John 13:34), He was trying to raise our thinking from what we need to do to what we need to become. It was not the commandment to love that was new, but the standard, or the quality and type of love. 'This is my commandment,' He said, 'That ye love one another, *as I have loved you*' (John 15:12; emphasis added). He was introducing a much simpler and yet far more demanding test of righteousness: 'By this shall all men know that ye are my disciples, if ye have love one to another' (John 13:35)."

"To keep us focused on this better path to perfection, Peter emphasized, '*Above all things*, have fervent charity among yourselves' (1 Peter 4:8; emphasis added). And the Savior prioritized, '*Above all things*, clothe yourselves with the bond of charity, as with a mantle, *which is the bond of perfectness* and peace' (D&C 88:125; emphasis added). This should help us to realize that the more we immerse ourselves in love, the more perfect we become.

"But what is charity? Mormon defined it as 'the pure love of Christ' (Moroni 7:47). I want you to think about that. Does he mean that charity is the love that Christ has for *us*? Or does it mean the love that we have for *Him* and His work? Who would be willing to explain what this means?"

There were several who volunteered. The president called on Elder Curtis, who said, "I think it means both. He shows His charity by manifesting His love for us, and we show charity by manifesting our love for Him by our obedience to His commandments and by loving and giving service to others."

"Thank you, elder. May I see a show of hands of those who agree with Elder Curtis?" It was almost unanimous.

"Now I would like you to ask yourselves, what are the characteristics, or manifestations of charity? How can we tell if we possess that gift?" Several hands were raised tentatively, but he ignored them and answered his own question.

"Both Paul and Moroni taught that one of the prime characteristics of charity is that it 'seeketh not her own' (see 1 Corinthians 13:5; Moroni 7:45). God, being the epitome of perfect charity, '*doeth not anything* save it be for the benefit of the world; for he loveth the world, even that he layeth down his own life that he may draw all men unto him' (2 Nephi 26:24; emphasis added). He has told us that His entire work and glory is to bring about the immortality and eternal life of man (see Moses 1:39). He does that every moment of every day, around the clock, around the calendar. Throughout the eternities, with no time off for vacations, He is ceaselessly and forever engaged in attending to our needs, for, 'he that keepeth Israel shall neither slumber nor sleep' (Psalm 121:4).

"But how does this apply to us and our charity? That commitment to care about and serve others is one of the attributes of charity that He wants us to seek on behalf of our fellowman. Jesus taught, 'Greater love hath no man than this, that a man lay down his life for his friends' (John 15:13). There is more than one way to 'lay down' our life. Giving love and service to others by giving our time and caring is a most important one. We are, for example, urged to 'be not weary in well–doing' (D&C 64:33) and that 'we should waste and wear out our lives' in building the kingdom (D&C 123:13).

"The more we are possessed of charity, the less we will do such things out of a sense of duty, and the more we will do them because we are filled with Christ's love—because we are becoming like Him and that is what He would do. Hopefully, here on your missions, you are learning to do just that with increasing willingness and joy."

That's exactly what I need to do, thought Elder Curtis. *No*, he corrected himself, *it's what I* want *to do. Rather, it is what I am going to do.* Once again he corrected himself. *No, it's bigger than that. It's the kind of person I will* become. His thoughts jerked back to the president, who was saying:

"As we wrap up this session, let's consider some of the results of obtaining the gift of charity. How will possessing charity affect our service as missionaries? How will it change our relationships? How will it improve us as disciples?

"Nephi described another aspect of the Savior's charity when he prophesied: 'And the world, because of their iniquity, shall judge him to be a thing of naught; wherefore they scourge him, and he suffereth it; and they smite him, and he suffereth it. Yea, they spit upon him, and he suffereth it' (1 Nephi 19:9). Why did He, the Creator of the universe, endure all that unjust treatment so willingly? The same verse explains that it was 'because of his loving kindness and his long-suffering towards the children of men' (1 Nephi 19:9).

"How can we apply that aspect of charity toward our missionary experiences? You may never give as many discussions as you hope for, but you can always teach something, even to people who rudely turn you away, by emulating this example of charity. You see, the more charity we have in our character, the less we will be concerned about how the actions of others affect *us*, and the more we will want to reach out to help *them*. Your *Preach My Gospel* manual describes how your discipleship will change as you receive more of the gift of charity. You have the quote there on your handouts. It says:

> You will come to feel a sincere concern for the eternal welfare and happiness of other people. You will see them as children of God with the potential of becoming like our Heavenly Father, and you will labor in their behalf. You will avoid negative feelings such as anger, envy, lust, or covetousness. You will try to understand them, and their points of view. You will be patient with them and try to help them when they are struggling or discouraged.[2]

"I know this is something you all want. And the beautiful thing about all this is that the more that you and I emulate charity in this way, the more we can assist the Savior in His work, as people will feel His love for them through us.

"Now, how do we obtain charity? We need to understand that charity is not something that can be manufactured by mortal human beings. It is a gift of God, and if we are to have it—in the fullest sense, as it is manifest by Christ—we must get it from God. Moroni taught that attaining these characteristics of the Savior's divine love is so important to our quest of becoming like Christ that we should 'pray unto the Father with all the energy of heart,' not to merely *obtain* or *have* charity but 'that ye may be *filled* with this love, which he hath bestowed upon all who are true followers of his Son, Jesus Christ' (Moroni 7:48; emphasis added).

The president paused a moment. As he looked directly at the sister who had asked the question, he cleared his throat and said somewhat reluctantly, "If you will pardon a brief turn back to this morning's discussion on perfection, may I mention that you will never read in the scriptures that you should 'pray unto the father with all the energy of heart' that you can be *perfect*. Perhaps that is because it is charity that 'is the bond of perfectness' (D&C 88:125) rather than the letter-of-the-law exactitude in keeping all the commandments, and 'except men shall have charity they cannot inherit that place which [God] hast prepared in the mansions of [our] Father' (Ether 12:34). No wonder Nephi testified that 'the love of God . . . is the most desirable above all things' (1 Nephi 11:22)."

Elder Curtis thought about all the reading and memorizing he had done prior to meeting with the president. He now realized that it was a subconscious attempt to substitute good works for the repentance he had been avoiding. Those were good things to do, but he had denied himself many blessings because his intent was wrong. He was so thankful he now understood that one cannot trade unrepented sins for good works.

President Love was saying, "Elders and Sisters, I would like to discuss this important doctrine with you further, but our time is growing short and we must allow time for interviews. I will conclude by saying this: Just as all the commandments are encompassed in our duty to love others, all sins boil down to a failure to love God, others, or ourselves. That being true, ultimately all our repentance should bring us closer to obtaining and emulating the gift of charity. As John admonished: "Beloved, let us love one another: for love is of God; and every one that loveth is born of God, and knoweth God. He that loveth not knoweth not God; for God is love. If we love one another, God dwelleth in us, and his love is perfected in us" (1 John 4:7–8, 12).

"I encourage you to study this doctrine further in your Bible's topical guide and in your *Preach My Gospel* manual under the headings of charity and love. You will find much to ponder."

The president ended by saying, "The zone leaders will inform you when it is your turn to interview. As you wait, they will lead you in some role-playing, skill-practice workshops. Thank you for your attention, and may the Lord bless us all in His work."

Elder Curtis smiled. He felt warm inside. All that he had learned about restitution, which is so necessary to repentance, was even clearer to him now. He now understood that regardless of the specific nature of anyone's sins, learning to show an increase of love toward God and one's fellowmen is a path of healing and of growing closer to the Savior.

NOTES

1 Bible Dictionary, 632.

2 *Preach My Gospel,* 118.

Permission to Proceed

hen it was Elder Curtis's turn for an interview, he entered and sat down, smiling at the president who smiled back but said nothing. So the elder began the discussion, which was exactly what the president was waiting for.

"President Love," he said, laying his three letters on the desk, "these are my confessions and apologies to my parents, bishop, and stake president. I have explained everything in full detail, with nothing held back. I have told them how sorry I am for deceiving them and how determined I am to make restitution by being an honest and faithful servant from now on. I am asking you to accept these letters as that part of my repentance without sending me home to do it in person. Will you please read them and tell me if that is acceptable?"

"Thank you, Elder Curtis, but I don't need to read them. Your accountability is to them, and if you were honest and forthright, then I trust what you said is sufficient. My concern is this: why did you choose to send letters instead of going home to do it face to face?" He watched the elder's face carefully. He saw only peace and determination. Elder Curtis's eyes met the president's with confidence. There was no squirming or looking down.

"President Love, I chose to send letters because the best way I can make restitution to them and, more important, to the Lord and the mission He gave me, is to stay here and become the missionary He expected me to be. If you feel I should go home, then I'll gladly do it. I'm not afraid anymore. But my feeling is that I can do more good by staying here and serving. I know that I am not as worthy as others, who came with more honesty and integrity in keeping their covenants. But I intend to become that type of person. If you will give me the privilege of staying, I will prove to you that I can and will live up to all that you have taught me."

The president was pleased. Elder Curtis had arrived at the same solution that President Hinckley, then an assistant to the Quorum of the Twelve Apostles, had recommended to a missionary in very similar circumstances.[1] Nevertheless, the president replied, "So what you are asking is that, after doing what you did, you want me to help you get away with it with no apparent consequences?"

With no anger or stress, the elder calmly replied, "No, that's not what I mean and that's not what I want. The consequences for my acts will follow me regardless of what you decide. I am going to make my life right with the Lord whether I stay here or you send me home. Either way, I am committed to follow the path of repentance as you have taught me. I will stay on the path of obedience and seek a closer relationship with the Lord wherever I am."

With obvious determination, Elder Curtis sat straight in his chair and continued: "All that I am saying is that I believe I can grow and improve and make a more meaningful restitution here, serving full-time, than I could at home. I am determined to have honor in my relationship with the Lord, and I would like to earn that here, before I go home. But," he added, "if Church policy won't allow that, then I will accept it, go home, and complete my repentance there. Either way, I was called, and now I am going to live worthy to be chosen." Smiling, he said, "I now realize that being chosen is not like passing a test or completing a checklist or acing an interview. If we are worthy to be chosen it will be because we, ourselves, chose to become enough like Christ that we will belong wherever He is, helping Him do what He does. That's the kind of person I am determined to become."

President Love was feeling good inside. This was the result he had worked and prayed for. He felt certain there was rejoicing in heaven above, as there was in his heart. "Elder," he asked, "if I accept your proposal, will you give me your word that, should you have any further problems with lust or unclean thoughts, you will immediately discuss them with me?"

"Yes, I will," he replied without hesitation.

"And you and I will have a visit every couple of weeks for the next few months, so that you can report to me on your progress and how you are feeling about yourself."

"Yes," he said, "gladly. There will never again be any effort on my part to hold back or hide anything from a priesthood leader."

"Then we have a deal," said the president, extending his hand as he stood.

"Oh," he remarked, sitting down again, "there is one other thing. My APs tell me that there are rumors and questions going around about you."

"Yes, that's true. A number of missionaries have already questioned me, but I wasn't going to say anything about it."

"What kind of questions?" asked the president.

"Well, some of them seem genuinely concerned that I'm okay and some of them are just being nosey and trying to get the details on someone in trouble. I'm not worried about that anymore. I found these two scriptures that I want to cling to for the next phase of my repentance. I've already memorized them. In the first one Jesus says, 'Thou art not excusable in thy transgressions; nevertheless, go thy way and sin no more. Magnify thine office' (D&C 24:2–3). In the second one He says, 'Behold, I do not condemn you; go your ways and sin no more; perform with soberness the work which I have commanded you' (D&C 6:35). That's what I am going to focus on. Let people think whatever they want to."

"That's a good attitude, Elder, but it is an issue that we need to deal with. People are always curious—that's just part of our nature. It is quite possible, if these rumors continue, that you could become labeled as the elder who almost got sent home. But there is an even greater concern."

Elder Curtis was surprised and exclaimed, "What could be worse than that?"

"Elder Curtis, even if others don't pin that label on you, there is a real danger that you will do it to yourself, so we need to talk about this for a moment. Do you remember who W. W. Phelps was?"

"Yes, he was a traitor. He was the man who betrayed Joseph Smith and the Saints in Missouri. It was his lies that helped put the prophet in prison and led to Governor Boggs's extermination order."

"Yes, that's true," replied the president, "but all of that changed when he repented. Did you know that he was also the man that wrote the hymn 'Praise to the Man?' "

Incredulous, the elder replied that he did not know that and wondered how it could be possible.

The president said, "The only way Brother Phelps could write such a song was if his self-image had been truly changed from one of a traitor to one of a regular, forgiven, and accepted disciple. How did that happen? And how can you make sure that you don't label yourself wrongly because of a past mistake?" He opened his Bible and quoted Paul. " 'Therefore if any man be in Christ, he is a new creature: old things are passed away; behold, all things are become new' (2 Corinthians 5:17)."

As President Love pulled another article from his briefcase, he said, "I want you to learn how to view and think about yourself and all other repentant people who you might work with in the future, as new creatures in Christ—not the way you or they were before repentance and forgiveness.

"This article was written by a colleague of mine, a former mission president, and he gave me permission to share it. He presents a powerful discussion on the proper way for a sinner to view himself after repentance, without applying self-deprecating labels. I think you will find it helpful in your own life, as well as others' whom you lead to repentance. Remember, Elder, the Savior's love and forgiveness are always bigger than any sin of which we are repentant."

He stood and shook hands again with Elder Curtis, who took the article, and then left with a very big smile on his face.

NOTES

1 See Sheri L. Dew, *The Biography of Gordon B. Hinckley*, 216.

Avoiding Negative Labels

*A*fter leaving his interview, Elder Curtis found Elder Jones, who was visiting with some other missionaries. Elder Jones could see the glow in his companion's face as Elder Curtis pulled him aside and told him that his problems had been resolved and that things would be better now. Elder Jones smiled and gave him a playful punch on the shoulder as evidence of his belief in him.

Since it appeared it would be a while before the interviews would be completed and they left the conference, Elder Curtis found a private corner and set about to study his final article, anxious to learn why he should not regard himself as "the elder who was almost sent home"—since that was most certainly the truth. He began reading:

Forgiving Oneself[1]
(By D. Chad Richardson, PhD, former Stake and Mission President)

At a recent stake conference, as the congregation sang the hymn "Praise to the Man," I thought about the composer, William W. Phelps. I was grateful for his hymns—15 in the current hymnbook—and for his love of the gospel and of the Prophet Joseph Smith.

I recalled how, during the trials of Missouri, he was reprimanded for misuse of Church funds and selling lands contrary to counsel. As a result, he became very bitter in Far West and turned against the Prophet and the Saints. Along with other apostates, W. W. Phelps was involved in an affidavit against the Prophet issued in Richmond, Missouri, in November 1838. After Governor Lilburn W. Boggs's extermination order, the Saints were driven from Missouri, while the Prophet and his associates were imprisoned for months in the terrible winter dungeon of Liberty Jail.

Elder Curtis paused and thought, *I was right about the betrayal. He was a traitor.* He continued reading, anxious to understand W. W. Phelps's transformation and how this would apply to his own self-image.

By 1840 W. W. Phelps had experienced a profound change of heart and wrote to the Prophet pleading for forgiveness. In response, Joseph's letter concluded with the couplet "Come on, dear brother, since the war is past, / For friends at first, are friends again at last" (see *History of the Church*, 4:163; see also 141–42). Joseph freely forgave Brother Phelps and took him back into full fellowship.

When Brother Phelps learned that Joseph and Hyrum had been killed by a mob, he was devastated. With great power and inspiration, he expressed his own feelings and those of the entire Church as he penned the hymn "Praise to the Man."

As we sang that hymn in stake conference, I was deeply moved by one line in the chorus: "Traitors and tyrants now fight him in vain" (*Hymns*, no. 27). How, I wondered, could Brother Phelps speak of traitors and tyrants fighting the Prophet when he himself had been one? Immediately I realized not only that Brother Phelps was no longer a traitor but also that he must have come to no longer see himself as one. The genuine, complete love and trust he received from Brother Joseph helped make it possible for him not only to forgive himself but also to erase his image of himself as a traitor.

We must keep sin in its proper perspective. Satan would convince us that we are defined by our sins. He would have had the repentant W. W. Phelps see himself always as a traitor. He would convince someone who has stolen that he is and always will be a thief.

The Savior, in contrast, would have us understand that we have sins that need to be cleansed, but we are much more than those stains. If I spill ketchup on my shirt, I have a stain. Perhaps it is right in front where everyone can see it. But while I have a stain, I am not the stain. I need to recognize that there is a good deal of my shirt that is clean and white. I believe that God sees the white shirt—the goodness in His children—and offers, through Christ, to remove the stains. If we obsess about the stain, however, it will become who we are in our minds and then in our actions.

Elder Curtis paused, feeling a very deep and satisfying assurance that repentance and forgiveness really do make a difference in how the Lord regards us and how we must learn to view ourselves. He rejoiced as he sensed that although his transformation was not yet complete, he was indeed on the right path, and with the passage of time and faithfulness, he too would become a "new creature in Christ." He continued reading.

Many years ago I had an experience that helped me understand the forgetting process. When I was very young, a man with a large, rather startling birthmark on his face moved into our ward. After some time, this man was called as our bishop, and he served during all my Aaronic Priesthood years. He was a wonderful bishop, and the members of our ward learned to love him dearly.

Years later, while I was attending BYU, someone vaguely familiar with the town where I grew up asked me who my bishop was. He didn't recognize the name I gave and asked for a description. I described his height, his hairline, his profession, and many other things about him. Then, suddenly, he asked, "Oh, is he the man with the big birthmark on his face?" I had to think for a moment and then said, "Yes, I guess he does have a birthmark." I was surprised at myself, for in my mind, the birthmark had disappeared. That simply had ceased to be an important part of who he was to me, though I could still remember if I tried.

When we turn to our Savior, He can heal us not only of the sin but also of the self-recrimination and the constant mental replaying of our sins or obsessing over them. We must turn the sins and the guilt over to the Savior in a process of complete repentance. For serious sins we will need the help of a bishop or another appropriate priesthood leader to complete our repentance. We then must let the Savior judge whether we or He must make final payment for the sin. Finally, we will need the Savior's help to feel self-acceptance rather than self-contempt.

With the Lord's help, we will experience a change in how we see ourselves. I believe this is the wonderful change that happened to Brother Phelps. Because of his repentance and his willingness to forgive himself, he was no longer a traitor. He was able to accomplish many great spiritual and civic works following the Prophet's death. I believe his accomplishments would have been highly unlikely had he not, with the help of the Prophet and the Lord, fully forgiven himself. Let us learn from his example.

As Elder Curtis thoughtfully placed the article in his backpack, along with his other treasured papers from the president, his desires expanded beyond becoming acceptable to the Lord to helping his missionary contacts and investigators. He rejoiced in the privilege to remain in his mission and teach other people about the truly marvelous "glad tidings" that he now understood more fully and was very anxious to share.

Notes

1 *Ensign,* March 2007, 30–33; used here with permission of the author and the *Ensign* magazine.

Epilogue

*S*ome months later, as the president sat in his office, his phone rang. It was his secretary, Sister Richardson. "President," she said, "I have one of your zone leaders on the line asking to speak to you."

He replied, "That's fine, I can take the call. Please put him through. Oh, by the way, which one is it?"

"It's Elder Curtis. He told me there is elder who is in trouble and thinks he needs to go home."

After the call President Love stood and read a framed poem on the wall.

The Beginning
By Steven A. Cramer

I heard the crowd before I saw it.
As I reached the top of the hill, I gasped.
Three men were hanging from crosses.
Blood was flowing from their hands and feet.

The one in the center was different.
His face was also covered with blood,

flowing from a crown of thorns.
But it was His calm serenity that held my gaze.
Why wasn't He screaming in anger and pain
like the other two?

His eye caught mine, and I knew
this was no ordinary man.
A charge of . . . of what? Awakening?
Challenge? Love? Invitation?
Whatever it was, it flowed through me and
I knew I would never be the same.

Suddenly His manner changed.
I wondered what He meant, and where He got the power
to shout: "It is finished."
Like the others, I trembled in fear as
the sun grew dark and the
earth shook beneath us—as if in angry protest.

When I looked again He was speaking softly,
reverently, to Someone unseen.
"Father, into Thy hands I commend My spirit."

Before I could question His meaning, He smiled at us
as if—as if He were leaving—just for a while.

He bowed His head, and I knew He was gone.
There was nothing left but the torn, empty shell.
And suddenly—I was lonely.

I turned to the man He had called John.
He was trying to comfort a sobbing woman.
"Excuse me, sir, but who was that man?"
"Come with us," he said, "and we will tell you."

The work had begun.

The president smiled with satisfaction. Elder Curtis would soon be
bringing him another confused elder. The work had come full circle.

Appendix A

More On Perfectionism

I have often pondered the mystery of how a perfect God could love us, just as we are, full of imperfection, sin, and weakness. For a long time I mistakenly believed that we had to somehow make ourselves good enough for God before He could accept us and love us. I am thankful to have learned that His love for us is not based on how *perfect* we are, but rather, on *who* we are—the children of God and the brothers and sisters of Jesus Christ.

I am also thankful for the encouraging words of President J. Reuben Clark, who reflected:

> I believe that our Heavenly Father wants to save every one of his children. *I do not think he intends to shut any of us off because of some slight transgression, some slight failure to observe some rule or regulation.* There are the great elementals that we must observe, but he is not going to be captious about the lesser things. I believe that his juridical concept of his dealings with his children could be expressed this way: I believe that in his justice and mercy he will give us the maximum reward for our acts, give us all that he can give, and in the reverse, I believe that he will impose upon us the minimum penalty which it is possible for him to impose.[1]

Brent L. Top, a BYU professor of Church history and doctrine advised, "To maintain a proper spiritual balance, we must remember that the Lord does not expect us to achieve perfection while in mortality. The unrealistic expectation that we must be perfect in all we do right now actually retards true gospel living and stifles spirituality. When we fall short of our preconceived notions of perfection, we tend to browbeat ourselves with undeserved self-criticism and guilt or to exhaust ourselves with unrealistic efforts to work our way to perfection."[2]

As we attempt to "lengthen our stride" and reach toward perfection, we must not confuse making rapid progress with being valiant. The strength of one's commitment to "endure to the end" is often more important than the pace of his growth. As Elder Marvin J. Ashton counseled, "The speed with which we head along the straight and narrow path isn't as important as the direction in which we are traveling. That direction, if it is leading toward eternal goals, is the all-important factor."[3]

There is great comfort in the Lords words, which give His assurance that the gifts and blessings of the gospel are "given for the benefit of those who love me and keep all my commandments, *and him that seeketh so to do*" (D&C 46:9; emphasis added). This shows us that in His infinite patience, what is most important to the Savior is not how perfect we are at this precise moment but the direction of our growth and where the desires of our heart are focused. As Elder Neal A. Maxwell assured, "Though imperfect, an improving person can actually know that the course of his life is generally acceptable to the Lord despite there being much distance yet to be covered."[4]

I take this to mean that even when we are imperfect in our present conduct but are sincerely trying to do better, God will show mercy as He weighs our righteous desires and efforts against our mistakes and weaknesses. As Elder Dallin H. Oaks stated, "When we have done all that we can, our desires will carry us the rest of the way. If our desires are right, we can be forgiven for the unintended errors or mistakes we will inevitably make as we try to carry those desires into effect. What a comfort for our feelings of inadequacy!"[5]

In the following words of Elder Bruce R. McConkie, I find strong confirmation of the forgoing ideas, as well as great hope for every member of the Church who is sincerely doing their best. Truly he shows that being chosen for exaltation in the celestial kingdom is within the reach of every temple-worthy member.

> Being born again is a gradual thing, except in a few isolated instances that are so miraculous they get written up in the scriptures. As far as the generality of the members of the Church are concerned, we are born again by degrees.... The same is true of being sanctified. Here again it is a process. Nobody is sanctified in an instant, suddenly. But if we keep the commandments and press forward with steadfastness after baptism, then degree by degree and step by step we sanctify our souls until that glorious day when we're qualified to go where God and angels are.
>
> So it is with the plan of salvation. We have to become perfect to be saved in the celestial kingdom. But nobody becomes perfect in this life. Only the Lord Jesus attained that state, and he had an advantage that none of us has. He was the Son of God, and he came into this life with a spiritual capacity and a talent and an inheritance that exceeded beyond all comprehension what any of the rest of us was born with. He lived a perfect life, and he set an ideal example. This shows that we can strive and go forward toward that goal, but no other mortal—not the greatest prophets nor the mightiest apostles nor any of the righteous saints of any of the ages—has ever been perfect, but we must become perfect to gain a celestial inheritance. As it is with being born again, and as it is with sanctifying our souls, so becoming perfect in Christ is a process.
>
> We begin to keep the commandments today, and we keep more of them tomorrow, and we go from grace to grace, up the steps of the ladder, and we thus improve and perfect our souls.... And so degree by degree and step by step we start out on the course to perfection with the objective of becoming perfect as God our Heavenly Father is perfect, in which eventuality we become inheritors of eternal life in his kingdom.
>
> As members of the Church, if we chart a course leading to eternal life; if we begin the processes of spiritual rebirth, and are going in the right direction; if we chart a course of sanctifying our souls, and degree by degree are going in that direction; and if we chart a course of becoming perfect, and, step by step and phase by phase, are perfecting our souls by overcoming the world, then it is absolutely guaranteed—there is no question whatever about it—we shall gain eternal life.
>
> Even though we have spiritual rebirth ahead of us, perfection

ahead of us, the full degree of sanctification ahead of us, if we chart a course and follow it to the best of our ability in this life, then when we go out of this life we'll continue in exactly that same course. We'll no longer be subject to the passions and the appetites of the flesh. We will have passed successfully the tests of this mortal probation and in due course we'll get the fulness of our Father's kingdom—and that means eternal life in his everlasting presence.

The Prophet told us that there are many things that people have to do, even after the grave, to work out their salvation. We're not going to be perfect the minute we die. But if we've charted a course, if our desires are right, if our appetites are curtailed and bridled, and if we believe in the Lord and are doing to the very best of our abilities what we ought to do, we'll go on to everlasting salvation, which is the fulness of eternal reward in our Father's kingdom.[6]

Let us close with the comments of Elder Joseph B. Wirthlin, who counseled: "Some may mistake the Church for a place where perfect people gather to say perfect things, think perfect thoughts, and feel perfect feelings. May I quickly dispel such a thought? The Church is a place where imperfect people gather to help and strengthen each other as we strive to return to our Heavenly father."[7]

NOTES

1 In Conference Report, 3 Oct 1953, 83–84; emphasis added.

2 "A Balanced Life," *Ensign*, Apr. 2005, 26.

3 "On Being Worthy" *Ensign*, May 1989, 21.

4 *The Neal A. Maxwell Quote Book*, 245

5 *Pure In Heart*, 79.

6 Bruce R. McConkie, "Jesus Christ and Him Crucified," *BYU Devotional Speeches of the Year*, 5 Sept. 1976, 399–401.

7 "Lessons Learned in the Journey of Life," *Ensign*, Dec. 2000, 7.

Appendix B

Addiction Recovery Resources

*B*ecause of the complexity and power of addiction to pornography, it would not be realistic in most cases (short of a divine rescue) to expect a person's willpower to enable them to stop "cold turkey" without the assistance of a dedicated and skilled priesthood leader, a therapist, or a twelve-step support group. The representation in this story was used solely for the purpose of creating a teaching opportunity.

If you have a loved one who is trapped in this or another addiction, please be aware that the Church Family Services Department is now providing an effective twelve-step recovery program. They are achieving wonderful results, both for those in addiction and for the support of confused and heart-broken family members.

It is always possible, through the aid of the Savior, for an individual to repent and recover from addiction without the aid of such a program. However, time and experience have proven that in many cases, working on such problems with the support of a group of fellow strugglers assisted by priesthood-assigned leaders and within the time-tested structure of the twelve steps, repentance and recovery are usually far more rapid and lasting. To locate the nearest addiction recovery program, call the LDS Family Services at 1-800-453-3860.

For a listing of books, cassette tapes, and websites that are helpful to those struggling to overcome addiction, as well as helping family members to better understand and support them, please review my website: www.geocities.com/StevenACramer.

Bibliography

Baker, Don. *Forgiving Yourself.* Portland, OR: Multnomah Press, 1985.

Bible Dictionary. Salt Lake City: The Church of Jesus Christ of Latter-day Saints, 1989.

BYU Devotional Speeches of the Year. Provo, UT: Brigham Young University Press.

Cannon, George Q. *Gospel Truth: Discourses and Writings of George Q. Cannon.* Selections by Jerreld L. Newquist. Salt Lake City: Deseret Book, 1974.

Conference Reports of The Church of Jesus Christ of Latter-day Saints. Salt Lake City: The Church of Jesus Christ of Latter-day Saints, 1898 to present.

Confronting Pornography. Edited by Mark D. Chamberlain, Daniel D. Gray, and Rory C. Reid. Salt Lake City: Deseret Book, 2005.

Curtis, Gerald and LoAnne. *The Worth of Every Soul.* Springville, UT: Cedar Fort, 2004.

Dew, Sheri L. *The Biography of Gordon B. Hinckley.* Salt Lake City: Deseret Book, 1996.

Doctrines of Salvation. 3 vols. Compiled by Bruce R. McConkie. Salt Lake City: Bookcraft, 1954–56.

For the Strength of Youth. Salt Lake City: The Church of Jesus Christ of Latter-day Saints, 2001.

History of the Church of Jesus Christ of Latter-day Saints. Period I. 6 vols. Edited by B. H. Roberts. Salt Lake City: Deseret News Press, 1902–1912.

Hymns of The Church of Jesus Christ of Latter-day Saints. Salt Lake City: The Church of Jesus Christ of Latter-day Saints, 1985.

Jensen, Andrew. *Latter-day Saint Biographical Encyclopedia.* Salt Lake City: Western Epics, 1971.

BIBLIOGRAPHY

Journal of Discourses. 26 vols. London: Latter-day Saints' Book Depot, 1854–86.

Lee, Harold B., *Youth and the Church.* Salt Lake City: Deseret Book, 1970.

Lewis, C. S., *Mere Christianity.* 29th edition. New York, New York: MacMillan Publishing Company, 1979.

Madsen, Truman G. *Christ and the Inner Life.* Salt Lake City: Bookcraft, 1978.

Maxwell, Neal A., *The Neal A. Maxwell Quote Book.* Edited by Cory H. Maxwell. Salt Lake City: Bookcraft, 1997.

McConkie, Bruce R. *Mormon Doctrine.* 2nd ed. Salt Lake City: Bookcraft, 1966.

Millet, Robert L. *Are We There Yet?* Salt Lake City: Deseret Book, 2005.

Oaks, Dallin H. *Pure In Heart.* Salt Lake City: Bookcraft, 1988.

Parker, William R. and Elaine St. Johns. *Prayer Can Change Your Life.* 17th ed. Englewood Cliffs, New Jersey: Prentice-Hall, 1965.

Salt Lake Institute of Religion Devotional Speeches. University of Utah. Salt Lake City.

Smith, Joseph, *Teachings of the Prophet Joseph Smith.* Selections by Joseph Fielding Smith. Salt Lake City: Deseret Book, 1976.

The Life and Teachings of Jesus and His Apostles. Church Educational System Course Manual. Salt Lake City: The Church of Jesus Christ of Latter-day Saints, 1978.

Index of Examples

Index of Quotations

Index of Terms

About the Author

Steven A. Cramer is the pen name for Gerald Curtis, author of more than a dozen books and talks on tape.

Since the release of his first book, *The Worth of a Soul,* in 1980, more than a quarter million books and tapes have followed, helping people rise from the defeat of weaknesses, bad habits, and addictions into the loving arms of the Savior by learning to apply the Atonement of Jesus Christ in their lives.

Professionally, Steven worked for the Postal Service, the aerospace industry, and in sales. In the Church, he has served in a variety of positions, including bishop and twice as a senior missionary with his wife, LoAnne Richardson. Steven now devotes the majority of his time to family history work. He and LoAnne have been married for over forty-eight years. They are the parents of nine children, and they have more than thirty grandchildren.